Lights i
& other stories

John F Bennett

The Lights in the Wood
and other stories

JoFra Press
www.jofrapress.co.uk

First published August 2020
©John F Bennett 2020
Second printing (with amendments) November 2020

Printed and bound in Great Britain by PurePrint Group
Crowson House, Bolton Close, Uckfield,
East Sussex, TN22 1PH
Tel +44 (0) 1825 768811
Fax +44 (0) 1825 768062

ISBN 978-1-5272-6858-6

Cover picture: ©John F Bennett 2020

Also in JoFra Press by John F Bennett:
The Girl on the Seventh Floor

JoFra Press
www.jofrapress.co.uk

publisher@jofrapress.co.uk
(Publisher and writers may be contacted at the above email address)

Dedicated to Claire, Gary, Chloe and Lucy

The Lights in the Wood

The cottage was where his parents and grandparents had lived their comfortable but drab lives; it was populated by the ghosts of his family and those who had inhabited the house before them.

To say he was unafraid was not quite true, although he was more concerned about the houses encroaching on his domain: on modernity and all it brought with it.

Cyrus – his ancient name befitted him – was nearly eighty, balding apart from a few grey strands of hair which he tended as a gardener tends a precious plant. His doctor proclaimed him 'in fine fettle' – whatever that meant – and he felt in the best of health, in good order. If that is what fettle meant he imagined his to be of the very finest.

'He could see off many half his age,' was his boast and his hermit-like existence fortunately ensured that he was never called upon to prove it.

Cyrus had been a winner in his life. He had stood alone – or so he claimed, ignoring the teams of poorly rewarded staff who built his fortune and his position. He believed he did not need friends, companions, neighbours – even to help him combat the less than friendly – there were some – ghosts who inhabited his cottage and its surrounds. Ghosts could be those of his past who had suffered by his greed and thirst for glory – although he largely discounted this theory since he had always managed to dismiss them from his thoughts.

Cyrus began to see the lights on a dark winter's evening: he had witnessed vague shapes before – even articulated figures - but never lights. He faced this new threat in his usual stoic way. He could believe that the ghosts were ancient inhabitants of his home; lights were quite different and more likely to be the product of a fertile human mind threatening his peace.

Cyrus had no car, not from principle but from a lack of necessity. His bicycle provided transport for where he wanted to go, and that did not take him beyond the lanes in the countryside surrounding his house. He was glad that this constituted a large area and that he could cycle many miles of country before the new town appeared to offend his eyes.

On his rides he could relive his business life when he had men to command, men who were unable to say no and unwilling to risk their futures by offering him offence. And they were good at what they did; otherwise his business enterprise could not have spanned the world, and his old age could not have been as comfortable as it was. He embraced new technology without ever needing to understand it; he put down his success to his ability to choose those who would realise his wishes. There were numerous pawns; *he* was unique.

And he was isolated in his home. Yes, his long suffering nephew had visited it to learn that he was his sole beneficiary, although Cyrus planned to reduce the amount of that bequest by expenditure on facilities to increase the comfort of the house he shared with his ghosts. But he was reluctant to risk the government taking too much of his wealth, so he planned that this would be limited by the recognition of his one living relative and his making of a will. And he continued to expand his land by purchase of farms around his dwelling – each acquisition bearing a higher cost owing to the competition from developers hungry for land by which they could expand the new town.

However Cyrus' nephew would still reap a rich harvest and perhaps he had deserved some recompense for the way his uncle had driven the young man during his uncle's time at the helm of his empire – and for the meagre payment with which he had rewarded him. Cyrus would chuckle in the comfort of his armchair: 'the boy' was not his equal (nowhere near that) and, again, he chose to ignore the value he and his colleagues had added to his own wealth. Somehow, the bequest was a reward for his nephew's patience, for he had received no additional financial help during the old man's lifetime – and Cyrus remembered the lack of belief his own father had had in him, and hoped that the acquisition of the bequest might be the making of his late brother's son. A desire for the family fortune - and business – to continue and thrive was strong.

When the lights began, he thought perhaps they belonged to a car straying beyond the nearest lane onto the tracks around his house. His concern lessened, strangely, as the appearance of the lights increased. But he was still intrigued by them and, one night when pinpoints of light appeared in the woods in which he would take winter walks, he chose to find their source. The darkness did not concern him; he took his own torch and its powerful beam would determine their origin.

Rain began as drops on the leaves: it did not deter him. As it became ever harder he felt assisted in his search: surely, if of human origin – which he was certain the lights were – it would lead him to a man or a group, drenched by the rain and sheltering in a clump of trees. He found no such source. But he proceeded into the wood, ever more determined. Until two lights flashed overhead – and gradually descended to the spot where Cyrus was. They continued to fall before him – and towards him. As they neared, he thought they would touch him.

Cyrus let out a cry. The lights had seemed to pursue him – or so he thought – and he fell to the ground. He regained his feet. The lights were gone. He had experienced naked fear, but not physical pain.

He stood and angrily drained the rainwater from his hat. The lights did not reappear but he had no desire to return to his search for their origin.

At the cottage, he bathed, dressed in clean clothes and

seated himself in his most comfortable chair. He began to read but found concentration difficult. Reading had not absorbed him but it had steadied him. He put down the book.

'Trickery,' he growled angrily; 'That's all it is.'

And he would resolve it. Why anyone should employ such measures he was unsure. The possibility that his ex-employees would resort to such trickery to gain revenge on him for his parsimony was soon dismissed. He believed he had paid his workers fair wages – comparable with the salaries they would have obtained elsewhere. If they believed they had been insufficiently remunerated, they could have left. No, he couldn't believe that was the answer. Could his nephew…? Unthinkable. Neither explanation could satisfy him. Cyrus sought, instead, a malicious source unknown to him – perhaps from those developers who sought his land. And the modern world had thrown up those who aimed at targets unknown to them – who delighted in the discomfiture (and more) of large numbers of computer users they had never met – even without attempting to make prospective gain.

There was, of course, the possibility of a supernatural explanation but it was not one which Cyrus entertained. He knew the ghosts that inhabited his cottage and there were few who caused him great concern, but even these he had long ago resolved to face, and believed they would not harm him. The majority even gave him a strange comfort: they were people like him. They were vindictive like him – but they shared his values and gave him, if not friendship, at least company.

He now believed that lights were different. Lights were the product of an age he could not understand. He had used its benefits; he had reaped the rewards it offered him – but he had done so through others. No, there was nothing to be afraid of. Even if he did not again seek out the lights in the wood, he would ignore them: they were not of supernatural origin. And, if a similar event which had occurred that night were repeated, it would not concern him. If 'they' had meant to cause his death by fright, their hopes would be unrealised. His nephew would have to wait many years for his bequest. If he used the bequest to further his family's fortune, so much the better but - Cyrus smiled – he would be in his seventies by the time he received it.

Cyrus was feeling better. He stretched, picked up his book and removed his bookmark. But he felt a minor sensation – which caused a pain in his chest. Before him, a small shape began to materialise. While he had seen many ghosts before, he had never received bodily discomfort on perceiving them. Perhaps the lights in the wood had frightened him more than he had thought?

He dismissed the idea. The ghosts themselves were probably only a figment of his imagination anyway. They had never harmed him – and *would* never harm him.

Gradually a figure took shape. There was something more worrying about that shape. No form had 'materialised' quite so quickly. Cyrus looked at the figure in awe. It was the apparition of his grandfather – the most ruthless and savage of his clan. And the shape was advancing toward him. Cyrus made to rise. Turning on the light would dissolve its form, perhaps. But he was unable to rise.

What had he done to his grandfather during the short overlap of their lives? He had certainly benefitted from his grandfather's building of the business empire, which came – with its considerable wealth – down to him through his father. But could his grandfather have felt envy, a feeling that his labours had benefitted others than himself? For he had not lived to enjoy the benefits of his labours; indeed Cyrus was the first in the family to reap dividends and build for himself a comfortable – if not homely – home.

Rejecting this absurd assumption, Cyrus had also dismissed the idea of a hologram illusion - he would not have described it as such but as technological trickery similar to the lights in the wood.

And, as his 'grandfather' – and he was convinced it was he – gained greater shape, the old man knew greater fear. He was fixed to his chair and could not rise, could not evade the inexorably approaching figure.

No ghost had done this before. No ghost had continued to approach before dissolving into nothingness. This wraith did not dissolve. Its shape became clearer. And, although it moved through the furniture in its progress, it appeared more solid with every step. And its face more and more resembled that of his deceased relative.

And its progress continued unhindered. It came on... and on. Cyrus gripped the arms of his chair and could feel an unearthly force rising in his body and to his chest, to his throat. The phantom leaned over him and his fear turned to an awful dread.

He screamed.

Cyrus was found in his cottage by his nephew. No cause could be found to account for his death. But what those who studied his body to find one could not help noticing was the look of cold terror that was etched on his face.

Bindy's Master Plan

'You don't do it that way.'

Maxie sighed.

'Well, do you want to know how to do it?'

'Go on then.'

'Well, you hit the ball like this and…'

'It goes out of court.'

'Well it did that time but I was talking about the principle; I was just showing you.'

'Thanks,' said Maxie, 'I'll know how to hit the ball out of court next time.'

Bindy stretched herself as high as her five foot five would allow her and glowered.

'Hit the ball to me.'

Maxie hit the ball.

'Hey, how can I hit a ball like that? It shot off to the left.'

'That must,' said Maxie, 'be the spin I put on it.'

'Alright, if you're not going to take this seriously…'

The tennis club assistant approached them:

'Time's up I'm afraid.'

Maxie walked off court while Bindy studied her watch and humphed.

'One hour,' said the assistant.

Bindy, too, walked off, unable to question his time keeping.

'Where shall we go now? Golf?'

'Are you an expert in golf?'

'Yes, I...'

'OK, we'll give golf a miss. The professional who coaches me may be annoyed if I get expert instruction from someone else. Everyone has a different method of teaching.'

Unaware of Maxie's irony, and secretly feeling that Maxie's 'professional' might not have the expertise to match hers, Bindy smiled:

'Yes, I suppose you're right. Best not.'

Stuart turned to his brother with the look of one who is smitten.

'Who is it?' Daniel asked.

'Haven't you seen her at the tennis club?'

'I've seen a number of very presentable girls at the tennis club.'

'Maxie.'

'Oh,' Daniel said with feeling, 'Maxie.'

It was unnecessary to ask if Daniel had noticed Maxie since it was clear that he had. Stuart thought that was unsurprising since everyone noticed Maxie. She was the sort of girl people noticed.

'I had thought...' began Daniel.

But the look with which Stuart responded suggested that thinking about Maxie, however little, was not a process he would tolerate.

'We are an "item",' he said.

'An item? OK.' Daniel left it at that and packed his tennis racquet in his bag.

The tennis courts were where Stuart and Daniel had met Maxie and Bindy, and they regularly played together, although the boys usually arrived much later than the girls, offering a period during which Maxie and Bindy could participate in what they termed 'girl talk'.

Maxie said: 'It looks like rain; it might put the boys off.'

Bindy raised her eyes: 'Put Stuart off?'

'Both of them.'

'Have you seen Stuart looking at you?'

Maxie had seen Stuart looking at her, rather more frequently than had Bindy, but shook her head.

'He's mad about you.'

Maxie showed no reaction.

'Absolutely mad about…'

Maxie held her hand up to indicate that she was unconcerned about Stuart's devotion and - Bindy believed – was unimpressed by it.

Bindy relished this lack of fervour. Although by no means unattractive, Bindy realised that Maxie received more admiring glances than her.

'Ah! I could help you. I am not inexperienced in the ways of the heart. Dealing with romance is one of my skills.'

Maxie was rather amused by the use of the word 'romance', although she knew Bindy to live in a world peopled by imaginary princesses living in towers to which handsome knights beat a relentless path.

'I have done it before and I can do it again. You could say I'm an expert in match making.'

'Or match unmaking?'

'Ah, well, in this case match unmaking.'

Maxie smiled but agreed that Bindy might play a part in dimming the light that sparkled in Stuart's eyes.

And, being Bindy's plan, it was soon to be put into practice.

'Just leave it to me,' she told Maxie.

'I will,' she replied guardedly.

'If things start to happen, just go along with them.'

'What sort of things?'

'Well, Daniel might invite you out.'

'And I am to accept?'

'You're getting the hang of it. Now, I will be guiding Stuart to you.'

'And that will help?'

'It will when he sees what you are doing with Daniel.'

'What will I be doing?' Maxie asked worriedly.

'You will be found in a compromising position.'

Maxie showed concern at how compromising this position might be.

'Oh, don't worry. Just kissing and things.'

'And things?'

'Oh, do I have to spell everything out for you? Just do your own thing.'

Maxie promised to do her own thing.

'With gusto.'

Maxie promised some gusto.

'Now we just need to plan where you're going to…'

'Compromise myself?'

'That's it.'

'With gusto?'

'Yes, with gusto; now I will be waiting with Stuart and we will see it all.'

'Not too compromising then?'

'We've been into all that; now listen.'

Maxie promised to listen, and Bindy set the time and place and went away to prepare her part in the plot.

Bindy had prepared the ground by suggesting to Stuart that Daniel had taken a shine to Maxie. Stuart's first reaction had been unpromising:

'Well I know that; I would expect it; she's lovely…'

'Yes, yes, but have you forbidden him to…'

'Well, I've warned him off.'

'Yes, that will do. Now, what if I told you he is going to ignore your warning?'

'He wouldn't…'

'Yes, he would. Come with me.'

Bindy led Stuart to an open space at which Maxie and Daniel had obediently begun to enact what appeared to be – from a certain angle – fervid love making. If the promised 'gusto' which Bindy had advised fell well short of her standards, she felt it would have to do.

She turned to Stuart:

'Would you trust a girl who could do that with your brother?'

Stuart said quietly: 'I think I will have to teach my brother a lesson.'

'No, no; just teach Maxie a lesson by never seeing her again.'

Stuart shook his head:

'If Daniel could do that...'

'But, if Maxie could do *that*.'

'Well, she is easily led.'

Bindy spun round: 'Easily led!'

It did not fit with her perception of Maxie's character.

Instead of bursting into a stream of invective against Maxie, Stuart moved towards the pair and took Daniel by the collar. His punch left a mark on his brother's cheek – sufficient to reflect the force of the blow.

Bindy, rushing to his aid, pulled Stuart away and put her arm round Daniel, holding up her hand to fend off the aggressor.

Stuart made no move to follow as Bindy helped the limping Daniel (although no leg injury had apparently been sustained) to the side of the open public area. Here they sat on a low wall and Bindy maintained her tight hold of him. Daniel, with apparent unconcern for his bruises, buried his head in her breast, feeling her hand tenderly stroking his face.

'Oh, my poor boy,' said Bindy, now stroking his hair.

She kissed his head and looked down as if on a favourite child. It was some time before she spoke:

'Do you think you'd be able to move?'

His capacity for movement should have been apparent to all but the besotted; however he showed little desire to move from the comfort of his position. Indeed he appeared to nuzzle further into that welcoming breast.

'Oh, Daniel, I never thought…'

Daniel looked up wondering what Bindy had never thought but the sentence was not completed. He regretted leaving the comfort of her embrace, for he had divined the missing words of her sentence anyway. She had never thought she was so fond of him. And, if Daniel could not bring himself to believe that, in such a short period, she had moved from friendship to love, he could at least see a considerable change in her attitude towards him. Could he believe that she loved him? He looked at her face. He believed it.

Meanwhile Stuart and Maxie were in similar accord. It lacked the intimacy displayed by Daniel and Bindy, but then they had known each other for longer and enjoyed an 'understanding' about which Bindy would have been amazed.

'I think I may have hit him too hard,' he said. 'But he did say to make it look realistic.'

Maxie looked across at Daniel, his head restored to its position on Bindy's breast, and smiled:

'I don't think you did,' she said.

'And did you enjoy your roll in the hay?' Stuart asked.

'Well, there was no rolling and no hay, but the performance – was it realistic?'

'Much too realistic.'

'Well, it was intended to appear that way and… Stuart I do believe you are jealous.'

'No, no,' he laughed and then, in a more serious tone, said: 'just don't do it again, that's all.'

But Maxie was thinking of Bindy:

'You know Bindy never gets it right. All her advice is incorrect; all her plans rebound but, although this plan went completely wrong, for once, as a result of her stratagem, everyone is happy.'

The Affair in Trenchard Street

Emmanuel Goodridge loved guns, not their look or feel, or their possibilities for sport. He belonged to a gun club but only because he could perfect the art of hitting a target. Not for the satisfaction of hitting a lifeless board but for the potential it offered for his main aim in life – to kill. Animals, yes, but principally humans.

He regularly viewed Internet sites constructed, and visited, by those who had similar interests and shared his grisly obsession. As one was closed down, another appeared. He was determined in his search for information and the possibility of contacting like-minded devotees.

He was unaware that his use of such sites, and his links with others using them, was leaving a trail of evidence should any-one seek to identify a killer. And a killer is what he was determined to be.

He knew that, if he was apprehended for a crime – and he admitted that he was unlikely to walk free from a killing spree – his neighbours would tell the newspapers and other media that he was a likeable man. They could not understand how that quiet man next door, or round the corner, could be a cold-blooded killer. Indeed they would fail to credit that he *was* – and disbelieve reports – how-ever steadfast his accusers had become.

How could someone who helped his neighbours on the rare occasions he spoke to them, or smiled so genuinely at them, be the type of man who had such a rare disregard for life? Of course, to Emmanuel, it was mostly an act – his 'quietness' resulted from his reluctance to associate with others; his apparent affability was as false.

It was Appleby – if he had a forename no one knew it – who put Goodridge on the right lines – if a path to perdition can be regarded as such. Appleby was a member of his gun club, but also an advocate of various sites which glorified in the sort of acts in which Goodridge revelled. And it was Appleby – evil, and therefore admirable - who made a suggestion that greatly appealed to his fellow aficionado.

Like many visitors to the sites they jointly visited, both saw ahead a killing spree which would make the sort of headlines they craved. But, where Appleby differed from Goodridge in approach, was that he advocated a shooting that would provide sufficient resources to be able to achieve that spree. And he had just the plan that would achieve that end.

They met at the gun club but spoke in clipped sentences which they hoped few would hear, much less understand. Appleby's plan was simple: Goodridge would shoot a man named Vintner who had been a criminal associate in a heist which had been so successful that Appleby described his associate's gain as 'a significant sum'. Appleby had not made a comparable sum although he admitted to being a smaller cog in the wheel. According to Appleby, Vintner had been able to give up crime and even acquire – apparently with the proceeds of the robbery – a measure of respectability. The advantage Appleby had over him – he told Goodridge - was that he knew where his erstwhile colleague in crime had secreted his 'earnings'. Appleby wished to obtain those earnings.

Appleby's plan could not have been simpler. Vintner would be shot – and Appleby would move in to secure the proceeds of the robbery, most of which he deemed rightfully his. Easy for Appleby. Goodridge's part in that plan was more difficult. Goodridge was to do the shooting. Whatever Appleby planned to do afterwards and - given that he had informed Goodridge that the police had no knowledge of the perpetrators of the crime – Appleby would be free to enjoy the fruits of it.

Goodridge had doubts – significant doubts:

'Why,' he asked Appleby, 'don't *you* shoot him?'

'Do you know what Vintner looks like, where he lives?'

Goodridge shook his head.

'Then you need me to lead you to him.'

'But, if you know him, you could…'

'I will be close to him to point him out.'

Goodridge knew he would be taking the greater risk, probably the only risk involved, and Appleby stood only to gain.

'And for your part,' Appleby continued, 'you will have half the proceeds.'

Goodridge was unconvinced. He needed time – time which Appleby assured him was unavailable. The money offered was significant and Appleby assured his colleague that half of it would be made available to him. Besides, he assured Goodridge:

'I'm not as good a shot as you are; I might miss. And, if you don't have a good sight, I can move him to where you could easily take him down. But, think of it, you will be a rich man.'

Goodridge, while still not happy, did think of it – although he also thought that, without his help, Appleby would be an even richer man. And, uppermost in Goodridge's mind was the exhilaration of committing his first shooting – getting on to the ladder of successful murders.

Goodridge would kill and see where it took him. He was able to locate a flat in Trenchard Street from which he had a good line to a pre-arranged spot where Vintner would be waiting, lured there by some tale that Appleby had concocted which meant that the two needed to meet. 'Leave that to me.'

Goodridge was sufficiently careful not to associate his name with the flat and was fortunate that it had been the home of an elderly man lately moved to a care home. And that it remained vacant. Acquiring the keys had been not been as difficult as he had anticipated, and moving his rifle with telescopic sights into a cupboard similarly simple.

Surprisingly Trenchard Street was quiet on the first day that an attempt was to be made. This was better than either man had expected. It ensured an easy sight for Goodridge and an easier opportunity for his escape after the shooting. It also made Appleby's task easier, given that, with only three people in the vicinity, and since he would, of course, be meeting Vintner, he did not have to risk himself to indicate Vintner's position.

As Goodridge watched, the three casual bystanders moved on. Appleby moved towards Vintner to justify the story of their necessary meeting.

Goodridge had already asked for a description of his intended victim, which had resulted in a vague response. To be certain (neither man had expected that Trenchard Street would be so deserted) he had also demanded to know what he would be wearing. Appleby had laughed at that:

'Well I don't think I will phone up and ask him, and I am meeting him, so I will be close to the man you have to target.'

Prepared and ready, Goodridge took aim.

Appleby fell dead on the pavement.

Goodridge did permit himself a wry smile. He collected his equipment and, having safely stored his sniper rifle, descended the fire escape at the back of the flats before the expected crowd gathered and the police arrived.

He negotiated the north end of Trenchard Street, risking a look back and noting that – unsurprisingly – Vintner was nowhere to be seen. It took a month of searching before he was to encounter Vintner again – his careful search of Appleby's house having revealed the details he required. A month which included sufficient time for Goodridge to ensure that he would not be apprehended in a place at which he should not be seen.

He made Vintner a proposition. A simple one. Division of the proceeds of the robbery or the revelation that the respectable Vintner had been part of an affair which did not accord with that respectability. Goodridge had expected fear on Vintner's part and a quick resolution of the matter. But his argument that he had proof that Vintner had taken part in a major robbery made that man smile.

When Goodridge appeared in the dock on a charge of murder, Vintner stood before him: Detective Inspector Vintner. That bastion of the law had reason to feel gratitude towards Goodridge. He had, after all, whatever his intentions, saved his life. Also, Goodridge had admitted that he was the assassin when he had tried to extract part of the proceeds of the crime he had believed Vintner to have committed. And, since proving Appleby guilty was the main problem that had faced the detective, Goodridge had also saved him the judicial process of bringing Appleby to justice: Appleby, to whom it had all seemed so simple to arrange the death of the detective whom, he knew, was close to arresting him.

A Long Texas Road

The road stretched dustily in front of them: straight ahead for as far as they could see. Artie settled into his seat. It could be a long time before they saw what they had come to see. The big Texan stared straight ahead, his index finger on the lowest part of the wheel, his mind apparently elsewhere.

'Where are the towns?'

The Texan glanced at his companion without answering.

'Where is Bakersville?' Artie persevered.

This the Texan answered:

'Passed it,' he said.

'But we've only passed two shacks on the whole of the journey?'

'Bakersville,' the Texan said drily.

Artie realised that their long ride would be largely unrelieved by conversation. However, he tried again:

'You must be rich, given the oil fields you own?'

'Yes,' said the Texan.

'Do you have land and…?'

The effort of conversation was too much. The Texan nodded without giving details.

Artie tried again:

'There was an obituary I read once in an English paper, *The Telegraph*, and it quoted the deceased as having told a story about his Texan friend. The Texan, to show his riches, had told him that he could drive for an hour without ever leaving his own land. The Englishman replied: "Yes, I had a car like that once".'

Artie awaited a reaction which did not come.

After the Texan had digested the story he said:

'Is that an English joke?'

Artie was surprised: 'Oh, yes, an English joke.'

The Texan's manner suggested that he did not appreciate English jokes.

Artie tried to stimulate what little conversation was likely to be made:

'I saw on a map that Lubbock is on this road.'

'West,' was the reply.

'Yes - a good way?'

'Far west.' The Texan replied.

'Buddy Holly was born in Lubbock. I'd like to go there.'

The Texan nodded to indicate that he knew about Lubbock, and said:

'The house where he was born isn't there now.'

'No.'

'No, the street is there but someone bought the house where he was born and moved it outside city limits. Nobody has been able to find it since.'

Artie derived from this information that absence of the actual birthplace rendered Lubbock somewhere not worth visiting. His dream of going to Lubbock faded.

And the Texan said: 'All this talking; do you want to be rich?'

Artie was unaware that conversation would prevent his being rich.

'Will I really be rich?'

'That's why we're going where we're going.'

There was a strong suggestion that he would not be accompanying this Englishman on such a long journey for any other reason.

'I've seen nodding donkeys. There are a lot of them.'

'There's lots of oil.'

'And you have oilfields?'

'A lot of oilfields.'

'How do you go about owning an oil field? You have to prospect for oil don't you?'

'You buy the land and then you apply for a drilling permit.'

'An exploratory well?'

'Yes.'

'The drilling permit allows you to drill? What if there's no oil?'

'There's oil,' said the Texan.

'Where do the permits come from?'

'Oil and Gas Division of the Railroad Commission.'

Artie looked puzzled: 'Why the Railroad…'

'I don't know,' said the Texan. 'It just is.'

'And the oil we drill for. There's big money in it?'

'Big money. Not quite as much as when I started – but it will still make you rich.'

Artie absorbed that, at least grateful that he had found a subject upon which the Texan showed interest – and about which he was willing to talk.

'And is there still a lot of oil to be found in Texas?'

The Texan looked suspiciously at Artie:

'You don't want to look elsewhere. I've got the land and I've got the drilling permit. It's all done. There's more oil in Texas than in Egypt or Malaysia.'

Artie pondered: 'More than Iran or…'

'There's a lot of oil,' said the Texan briefly.

'And why do you want me in on it?'

'Because you want to be in, and I've got big expenses.'

'Even with your land?'

'You can't exploit oil with land.'

'And other wells?'

'And other wells. The more oil, the more capital is needed: the more the profit you make. That's where you come in - with your lottery win.'

'Yes, I told you about that. Well, I'm grateful and I'm in.'

The Texan did not react. He was confident in Artie.

'I have to go back to England tomorrow, so I'll need to sort things out.'

'We'll sort things out.'

The car travelled another fifty miles before the driver stopped.

'There!' he said.

'But there are no nodding donkeys?'

'Of course not, that comes later.'

'No drills.'

'No drills yet.'

Artie looked around. Although the land was just a parched field, nodding donkeys, as he called them, stretched ahead. 'Where are we?' he asked.

'Hasn't got a name. Doesn't need a name… yet.'

'Well, you obviously know all there is to know… And you've got a permit?'

The Texan showed Artie a piece of paper which had a sufficiently official appearance to convince him; anyway he nodded.

The Texan showed him oil production figures – a mass of graphs – which he said indicated the progress of his other wells.

'So what do you need from me?'

'Transfer your investment and I'll give you a receipt.'

'I'll need a receipt.'

'You'll get one. You said you had your computer; I don't use them much.'

Artie took his laptop from its case and keyed the website address of his bank – and entered his ID number and password.

The Texan glanced but gave it little more interest: 'I have my account details,' he said.

Artie took the printed details and began to type:

'Right, that's my sort code; you don't have sort codes in The States, but you have an equivalent to show which branch you bank at.'

The Texan looked up sharply: 'So, you can tell where my bank is?'

'No, it's just a jumble of numbers.'

He continued to type.

'That's your account details. Now, if you just leave me to finish off this transaction. Remind me of the figure to be transferred?'

Artie gasped.

'I know it's more than we discussed,' said the Texan. 'But costs are going up all the time and…'

Artie returned to his typing: 'OK,' he said, 'I understand.'

Artie clicked 'Continue' and then 'Confirm'.

'All done,' he said.

Since all hope of Lubbock had been forgotten, he asked:

'Would you take me back to Dallas?'

'Airport?'

'Not yet, I'm staying in Dallas, leaving tomorrow.'

In England, Artie had ample time to search for details of oil procedures in Texas. He was able to search the land registration department of the State of Texas for details of land ownership under the Texan's name.

There were none.

He searched for details of prospecting, discovery and drilling for oil and they were much as the Texan had told him in his long drive from Texas; in fact *Wikipedia* even cited the examples of Egypt and Malaysia which the Texan had also mentioned when comparing oil output to Texas.

There was still the search for the Texan himself – never an easy matter. However he had his name and, as a major oilman, he should surely find a good return from Google. He did not; it caused him to contact his friend, a solicitor with expertise in this area. For Artie needed, he felt, to notify law enforcement in the State of Texas. His over-simplified view that one contacted the local sheriff, who set the wheels in motion, produced a smile on the solicitor's face, but he then frowned:

'You are beginning to fear that this was all a scam aren't you?' he said.

'Not beginning… I was quite convinced by him – or whoever helped him - during the correspondence we exchanged before I went to Texas, and after I'd made the lottery win,' said Artie, 'but, as soon as I met the man, I knew he was trying to scam me.'

'But the sum you mentioned was massive. You must be very worried now?'

Artie smiled: 'Having his car registration number – if it was his car; his bank details and the paper he gave me (rather stupidly – he should have flashed it at me) with his address at the bottom, we should be able to trace him. And, besides, there are very useful boxes on an on-line bank transfer form: "transaction name" and "payment reference". I filled in his bank details there, and, in the relevant parts of the form which effected a transfer, my own details. So I transferred the money from one of my bank accounts to another.'

The Manor House

It was easy to stumble in the mist. I felt myself falling onto a hard surface, but I knew I must rise. This was no place to stay.

I pushed myself up, easing my leg; the pain was considerable but there was more about which to worry. I looked around, as far as I could see through the mist, and realised that I was lost. What is more I had encountered some sort of dwelling – not a homely cottage which was likely to house a welcoming family who would take me in – the mother tending to my leg, the father preparing for me a place by the fire and telling me the path I must take… Not that sort of house. Indeed, I wondered if it were a dwelling of any sort. Perhaps it had been, but this part of it, at least, was now clearly a ruin. Why, I wondered, had I never seen these ruins on my previous walks?

I looked down at what had caused my injury, brushed away the encroaching foliage of ages and saw – a cherub. A stone cherub. And, investigating the area behind it made me certain that the cherub had once been mounted on a stone pillar. Just to the right was its companion. A pillar and another cherub.

I wondered if what I had found was a church; I was not aware that houses sported cherubs as decorations. I could be mistaken. I did not know much about old houses. I walked, slowly, taking the strain on my right side to assist my progress on the injured leg. I peered through the bracken, and made my way between entangled weeds, adding to my discomfiture by pressing on through nettles, brambles and the twigs of trees.

I was looking for more signs of the ruin I had encountered. Could it have been a folly, an outhouse? Could it be the remains of a house which had long since disappeared? For no mansion appeared ahead. My stumbling progress brought me into contact with more concrete remains and my arrested movement made me increasingly aware of them. There was a shield. I looked more closely – a coat of arms. A lion rearing up, above a crown: the crest of a family which would, if it had not already, achieve prominence in the land.

But I did not think of these things at the time. It was the knowledge that I was lost, and miles from home, that convinced me my return journey would be a painful one.

I discovered more fallen masonry, more figures and another crest, similar to the first. I struggled over it and, there, among the trees, was a structure which the ruins had not prepared me for. Indeed I was surprised that I had not previously been aware of the house, so massive was it. Had the trees through which I had passed really obscured it? I doubted that.

Despite feeling disorientated, lost and frightened, I felt a pull towards the house and succumbed to its attraction. Its condition was immaculate. It was clearly old but the miserable masonry in the tangle of weeds had led me to imagine that the house, if it proved to exist, would be in an advanced state of decay.

I continued to let the house's magnetism draw me on – and into it. I passed through a great, oak door without my progress being hindered. I was greeted by darkness and silence. If inhabited, where were the occupants? And why had an edifice on such a scale been hitherto unknown to me?

I banished these thoughts and sought the people who lived in the mansion. But I saw no one and the darkness oppressed me. Through none of the windows had a light shone, leading me to the assumption that the house was unoccupied, perhaps that it had been deserted – although the condition of the hallway did not suggest that the desertion had occurred during the distant past.

And neither did the interior into which I peered show

signs of having been long vacated. I was expecting unkempt rooms, the dust and dirt of ages: I found, instead, a house which was clearly lived in, its furniture showing signs of age perhaps but not of desertion. I moved into a long room, looking like a gallery, lined with portraits and with occasional tables set against the walls. I passed through it and saw a room which had clearly been used as a dining room – perhaps, given the glinting cutlery and food vessels upon it, it still served that purpose.

There was no food, which was not be expected, but it would not have surprised me to see an army of servants entering and beginning to load the table with food vessels and soup tureens.

But, as I looked up as if this vision might appear, another met my eyes. I reeled from the sight of a figure all in white. I crouched behind the table and peered round its leg at the newcomer. She was dressed – for it was a woman – in a long dress which covered her body from her neck to her feet. I could see that her feet were bare. The diaphanous garment, its lightness combined with her slim body, gave the girl's progress the appearance of the movement of a spirit. But spirit she clearly was not. Her lithe body moved forward with a graceful motion, her dress rippling with her movement.

Her mesmeric affect upon me had made me forget my caution. I was now standing in full view of her – but she clearly could not see me. Although the figure's appearance unsettled me, I felt compelled to move closer - but she remained unaware of my presence. I was a visitor to her world and not she to mine; I was a spectator in a parallel universe to my own.

There was about her an appearance of apprehension. I approached her with a view to providing assistance, but she continued to study the doorway. It was a direction in which my eyes also turned. And, suddenly, we were both startled by the entrance of a man – dark-browed and brooding, his eyes showing hatred and aggression.

She moved but was not quick enough to escape his clutches and he grabbed at the dress, pulling her back and tearing its material. With one movement, he easily lifted her, holding her under her neck and knees so that her head flopped back and her bare legs dangled. He carried her in this fashion towards the doorway of the room.

I noticed her haunted, terrified expression, and followed her attacker with great difficulty. My injuries had already made quick movement arduous, but my pursuit was also hindered by a heaviness of body which was new to me. All I could do was to force my body forward so that I could, at least, keep within sight of them. The girl's screams echoed around the building as he proceeded along a corridor to a room with a heavy door decorated with studs. Here he entered with his burden. Although the door was only slightly opened, I was able to see him throw the girl onto a bed where she curled into a defensive position. But his anger had subsided and, with a look of contempt at her, he withdrew from the room and slammed the door, turning a large key. Proceeding along the corridor, his task accomplished, he disappeared round the corner at its end. I tried to follow but my legs were weary, and I was unable to match his speed.

I turned back to the room in which his lady was incarcerated and peered through the keyhole. I was surprised to be able to see a small bare prison with only a bed. And, on that bed, was the lady in white, uncurled from her previous position, but still with a numbed, hopeless expression.

I spoke through the keyhole, keeping a wary eye on the corridor to ensure that the man had not returned. At first I whispered to her and then, abandoning caution, shouted through the keyhole. She did not move. I shouted louder but, although she stirred, I knew that it was not in response to my voice. I continued to talk but she never looked towards the door, only to the floor, at her poor, bare feet which must have been frozen in that cold house. She drew her legs up under her and sat, staring vacantly at the wall, at a prospect I was unable to see.

I was tired, very tired; my leg was giving great pain and I remembered that I was lost. I needed to try to make my way home, but I was reluctant to leave the lady whose beauty filled my mind and whose predicament fuelled my fear. However, I could not assist; she was unaware of my presence and I was unable to penetrate the walls of her prison.

With the greatest reluctance I began to make my way back down the corridor and into the dining room, before turning into the long gallery. I tried, unsuccessfully, to comfort myself with the thought that I would plan her escape and return to put any plan I contrived into operation.

But, for the present, my problem was how to exit the house. The huge front door, through which I had passed so easily, was now firmly locked and I investigated windows and other means by which I could leave. Eventually finding, to my surprise, an open window I continued into the wood through which I had originally approached the house.

Past the stone coats of arms and fallen cherubs, I walked in a direction by which, it seemed to me, I had entered the wood. The mist had cleared but now darkness was my enemy. I walked as rapidly as my leg would permit, taking time only to look over my shoulder for any unlikely pursuit. But I could not see the house any more than when I had approached it. I then suddenly heard a welcome sound, that of a car's engine. A moving car meant a road and a road would help me to determine my location. The car was some way off by the time I had reached the road, but it was coming in my direction. I stepped into the road and waved both my arms, hoping that its driver could penetrate the darkness with his beam.

And he did. I pulled open the door.

'I need to get to Mansing.' I told him.

He nodded and, without speaking, took a book off the seat so that I could sit down. I sat and expressed my gratitude to him, although he showed no reaction, his face still staring at the road ahead. I was unable to see his features.

Then, since he appeared to be oblivious of my presence, I took the liberty of picking up the book that rested on the ledge in front of me: an interesting looking book, its brown pages and calfskin cover indicating its age. For some miles it remained on my lap without my opening it, for I was aware of my lack of courtesy to the driver in handling it at all. I was, also, now somehow aware of his disapproval of my action.

I began to see sign posts to familiarly named villages and, at last, one directed the driver to Mansing. At this point, knowing that the driver and I would soon part, I looked to see what the book on my lap contained. But I hastily closed it, the driver, for the first time, looking towards me. As I turned to face – and thank him – I was drawn to his dark and sinister features. I hastily thrust the book back onto the ledge and reached for the door catch.

It was the face of the man I had seen in the house.

Having rested, I rose from my bed and looked at the leg that I had injured the day before. To my astonishment, it had ceased to give any pain and I could put all of my weight on it without discomfort. While I was relieved, I could not believe that, if suffered in this world, it was an injury which would have healed so quickly and so completely. I turned to my plans for the day. Firstly I needed to establish the location of the house in which I had experienced such strange events the day before. For a moment I began to doubt that it had all actually happened – perhaps I had dreamt my encounter with the beautiful lady in white and her warder.

But it had been too vivid: there was no possibility that it had not actually happened.

My first task was to find a map. I knew that I possessed a large-scale Ordnance Survey map of the district and I opened it flat upon the table. I traced, as far as I could, my progress on leaving home and the point at which I left my normal path. Even if the house were now ruined, and my experience indicated that it was not, I expected to see signs of it on the map.

There were none.

I folded the map, realising that I must seek an older map and, for this, I needed the reference library in Mansing. Although this was not a major reference section, I expected to find older OS maps and was not disappointed. However, the disappointment came when I inspected them and found no indication of the existence of a large house, or remains of any kind, anywhere near the route I had taken.

My disappointment must have been apparent since the member of staff who had found the maps for me came over to enquire its cause. When I explained, she looked puzzled:

'Old manor house?'

'Or similar. A stately home?'

'Oh, yes, of course, but this is only a small reference collection; you need to search even earlier maps to find it. Nothing of the manor house has existed for hundreds of years,' she said.

'I'm the secretary of the local history society, and the expert on that house is one of our members: Mr Mainwaring Faulds. He has lived in the area a lot longer than I have and he has earlier maps but, more importantly, considerable local knowledge.'

I smiled, thanked her and hoped that the estimable Mr Mainwaring Faulds would have some knowledge that, I was beginning to realise, was lacking elsewhere.

The phone rang:

'I think we should meet.'

I hardly needed an introduction to know that I was speaking to Mr Mainwaring Faulds, the possessor of local knowledge. And I was very happy that, instead of denying all knowledge of the mansion, he was suggesting a visit to his house, where I would find, amongst his treasures, an item which was relevant to my search. I also discerned from our conversation a considerable interest in it, and that he would find a conversation with me just as illuminating as I with him.

Mr Mainwaring Faulds somehow fitted the impression I had formed of him. Thin white hair cascaded down his face, which he constantly brushed away from his eyes. His likeness to Einstein was not entirely superficial and his enthusiasm when talking about his 'artefacts' enhanced that impression.

But he was aware that, as much as I should have normally shown – if not have felt – an interest in his samples of Samian ware, my only reason for visiting related to my recent enquiry.

We passed into a room which, to my disappointment, contained relics of the area but no pictures of the house which I – and I believed he – had seen.

However, as he took down a volume from his bookshelves, I felt a charge of enthusiasm difficult to describe. He could see my reaction and his eyebrows were raised in interrogation.

'You have seen it before?'

'Briefly,' I answered, telling him, for the first time, the story of the man in the car, and the book, which I was now seeing for the second time.

'Ah, yes, dark features, heavy brows, fierce countenance?'

I could not claim to have studied him so closely, although one look had been enough to hasten my rapid escape from the car - and the description certainly fitted.

'Did you talk to him?'

I hadn't done so, other than expressing my gratitude. I looked at Mr Mainwaring Faulds, realising that his enquiring mind would not have reacted in so feeble a fashion.

'Where have you seen that face?' I asked, perplexed.

In answer he reached for the volume that was, by now, in my hands, and opened it at what I realised must be a significant page.

There, to my amazement, was a plate showing the house and, below it, the face of the man I had seen in it.

'I suggest you read this,' he advised.

I needed no encouragement but sat on one of the few chairs and turned back the pages to where the chapter began. The story was one of evil, of a man whose determination to acquire position had led him to the incarceration of the woman he had married in passion and with whose company he had chosen to dispense.

Undoubtedly the portrait showed the man in the house –

and his likeness to the driver of the car was uncanny.

'I think you have had a remarkable escape,' Mr Mainwaring Faulds told me.

I wondered why. How had the driver known that I had just left a house which did not exist and had had such a profound effect on me that I was anxious to engage in research into its occupants?

'The path from which you emerged leads nowhere,' he said, 'and the majority of your experiences would have been etched on your face. They have not left it now.'

I began to turn the page.

'I do not want you to consider too seriously the conclusion the book draws.'

I must have appeared puzzled.

'There were many copies of this book,' he explained, 'but all were destroyed – except one. I have always assumed that I held the only copy. Clearly there may be another.'

He hesitated and further perplexed me by saying: 'Perhaps there is no other.'

'Have you any objection to my reading on?'

'I am not preventing you, certainly not; indeed I encourage you to do so. However, even the author of this work had to use his imagination in finishing the chapter. I do not know, and I am certain the writer did not know, how the story ended. So far you have read about the owner of Mansing Manor, who had married your lady in white but subsequently felt a stronger motive for marriage: to enhance his position in society.

'He had married, in a moment of passion, a beautiful village girl. His caution, even then, had led to his keeping the union secret.

'All that is recorded is that the Lady Beacham, eldest daughter of the Earl of Fletching, married this merchant. As far as he was aware no one else knew the marriage to have been bigamous.

'And, now, while the author of this history of Mansing records that the wife – your lady in white – was quietly removed from this world, I am sure that this was not the case. I am sure…'

'That she lived?'

'That she lived.'

'But why did he imprison her rather than…'

'This was before his second "marriage". He had not, at that point, convinced Lady Phillida that union with him was a sensible choice – after all, rich as the house's occupant undoubtedly was, he was, otherwise, no great catch. His reputation was as an inveterate gambler, suggesting that perhaps his fortune might soon be dissipated.

'But why do you doubt the end of the story?'

'Well, that is for you to tell me.'

'But I have discovered nothing to prove that "my" lady did not die.'

'And I am not totally convinced that she did not, but I wish to know for sure – and, although I have seen the manor house as you have, I have not seen its occupants. It seems you have a second sight even more intense than mine.'

Mr Mainwaring Faulds had been convinced that, if I took my original path, I should re-discover the house. And the following day I sought it again. I encountered the stone cherubs and the coats of arms. On this occasion I withdrew a notepad that I had deliberately taken to sketch the heraldic symbols. Passing on I saw again, as my companion of the day before was convinced I should, the manor house which had, for so long, shielded its tragic secrets.

And it was unnecessary, this time, to enter the house because – on my entrance to its wooded grounds - appeared a woman: 'my' lady. As she passed me, I could see her face and the look of abject terror which appeared on it. I called to her but, as I expected, she was unaware of my presence.

As she disappeared through the trees, I caught sight of her pursuer and his identity, too, failed to surprise me. The man whose portrait had appeared in the book, whose glowering face I had seen on my last visit and, perhaps too, on my journey home.

As he passed, just feet away, I lunged at him to hinder his pursuit. As I should have guessed, it did not do so and his progress was unimpeded. However, as he ran to the place in the trees through which the object of his pursuit had vanished, his foot caught a tree root and he fell. For a few moments, I stared in disbelief, which turned to delight as I realised that his knee was dislocated, and his chase was over. For the moment at least, 'my' lady was safe. I ran on but I could not find her. 'My' lady had vanished and I was never to see her again.

The next day I renewed my acquaintance with Mr Mainwaring Faulds but in strange circumstances. My knock at the door was answered – but not by the man I sought. Instead, in front of me, stood the man who had been driving the car. Although his features were similar to those I had seen that night, and there was no question that it was the same man, the smile on his face lightened his looks – to the extent that I accepted his invitation to enter.

I could not forget Mr Mainwaring Faulds' concern that I had been in danger by being his passenger but, somehow, I could not believe that this man, as he smiled at me, was capable of any evil act.

From another room, Mr Mainwaring Faulds appeared, with a worried look on his face, as if concerned for my welfare. I was politely requested to sit, which I did, and told them of my visit to the grounds of the manor house.

'Somehow,' said the white-haired man, 'I thought something like that had happened. You do not surprise me.'

And then he introduced me to the man who had answered the door:

'Meet,' he said, 'my cousin – George Mainwaring Faulds.'

I continued to walk around the area near the manor house for the comfort it gave me and, on one of my walks, I met a girl. She was dressed all in white, with a dress which came to her ankles – and, to fit with my recollections, she wore nothing on her feet. It was presumptuous of me to speak to her but I had to do so – indeed it was difficult for me not to touch her to ascertain whether she was 'my' lady – she exactly resembled her – and whether she belonged to this, or another, world.

But her answer to my greeting told me: she was flesh and blood.

I found it hard to engage her in conversation. How does one talk to the image of a girl so similar to one who had occupied my thoughts for so long?

But the few words we exchanged were merely a prelude to a relationship which developed with the weeks into a burgeoning romance. How could I do other than love her?

My only two worries, when I was with her, were the dreams which too often disturbed her sleep – and our sense of being watched when we walked.

She could not explain why she was drawn to those wooded paths despite the menace the woods seemed to hold. I had not told her of my experiences of the manor house, and neither had she revealed any knowledge of it. But, as our relationship began to grow, so did my distrust of George Mainwaring Faulds. I had received a phone call from his cousin who had explained that, although they rarely met, he knew only too well the danger posed by his relative:

'He is on the verge of insanity,' he had said, but then hesitated: 'No, he *is* insane. He has an obsessive interest in the family. He believes, after all this time, that he needs to defend its honour, not that I am aware that our family can ever claim to have been honourable. I am not going to say any more, but you need to be very careful and to keep your young lady away from him.'

I had resolved, even before this, to prevent George seeing the lady who so closely resembled she who, I now felt sure, was the descendant of *his* ancestor's wife.

Her nightmares continued. Much as I tried to comfort her, her night terrors would affect not only her nights but also our days.

But our walks continued. The delight in them was affected by the knowledge – it was no longer merely a feeling – that we were observed. And one morning I saw the face that I was dreading to see. I was unsure whether its features were those of the monster who had maltreated 'my' lady, or those of the polite and very much alive, George Mainwaring Faulds.

I had, for some time, considered the matter of the watcher in the woods. I could no longer believe that the subject of the chapter in *The History of Mansing* somehow still existed – other than as a man I had encountered in some sort of parallel universe. And George Mainwaring Faulds could surely have no reason to inflict harm on the lady with whom I walked. Unless, that is, there was a feeling on his part that her ancestor had tricked his family – and was a witness to the fact that the marriage with nobility had been a sham? And unless revelations of the past would affect his reputation in the district.

Could that really matter to anyone today? The man I had seen in the manor house had, according to the conclusion of the chapter in *The History of Mansing*, wasted the wealth his ancestors had accumulated – so he had not, as he had intended, used his marriage as a route into the aristocracy. Anyway, no one, surely, knew the story, since it was now clear that there was only one extant copy of the book, which was shared by the cousins. The mansion pre-dated recent maps of the area and records would, though they clearly existed, have been very difficult to locate.

But the man who glared at us through the trees - George Mainwaring Faulds – showed again the scowling features of his ancestor and the person his cousin had described. I could now quite believe in his insanity. He resented my lady's, and now my, presence in this world, and was determined to rid it of us. In his hand was a knife, long enough and sharp enough to achieve that end.

As soon as he started forward, I lifted my lady in a fashion I had seen his ancestor do. It did not occur to me until later just how similar the hold had been to that which I had witnessed in the manor house and, for the moment, my only thoughts concerned our escape and the preservation of her life.

His pursuit was swift but, in uncannily similar fashion

to his ancestor's accident, George Mainwaring Faulds had fallen, with a cry of pain, onto his knife. My haste was now unnecessary. I looked back to see him lying on his front, the knife projecting from his side.

Although the *Mansing Gazette* later ran a story of his 'tragic accident', I was, at the time of the incident, unsure that it had led to his demise. So I had not relaxed my hold on the lady whose transposition from her ancestor was now complete.

I looked down at her, knowing that her nightmares would no longer trouble her. I kissed her fondly. The experience which had begun at an indeterminate time, in a place which no longer existed, had culminated in this moment.

Nothing is Impossible

Grayson was an author. At least, he wrote books. They encompassed 180 pages each – a reasonable length – and Grayson was satisfied that they were fine. Good books. Great books. They might be discovered many years – perhaps even hundreds of years – hence. But, for now, they had never achieved that vital stage: publication. They had never troubled a printer despite Grayson's attempts to inform publishers of the riches their appearance on the book stands would achieve for them.

Yes, he could send them to an Internet publisher; yes, he could pay to have them published. Neither route was the way Grayson's work should appear before the public, or the few readers who would seek them out.

But Grayson was neither naïve, nor foolish. His work was well constructed and soundly researched: it used his own experience of working in a research laboratory. And he was surprised that real villains took fewer pains in planning their crimes than he devoted to his books – after all they had more to lose from their failure to do so. Why, for instance, did criminals avoid simple precautions? Oxygen bleach will remove DNA from a crime scene – and a spray comprising multiple samples of DNA will create sufficient confusion to prevent discovery of the criminal's. Perhaps this, he thought, was a little more difficult to obtain – for someone not working in such a research establishment as that in which he was located every day of this working life.

Most criminals were now aware of the need to wear gloves. A good proportion of earlier crime novels had been solved with the discovery of carelessly left finger prints. None of his criminals were so easily brought to book: his novels combined realism with imagination and painstaking research. His latest novel – he refused to believe a reputable publisher would resist the appeal of his plots for ever – was being prepared for the firm of Nicholls & Brent. He had heard that they welcomed new fiction, were appreciative of well-worked story lines and marketed and presented their books in a way which would satisfy Grayson's desire for immortality.

The use of realism, Grayson believed, was his greatest merit. He spent more time than perhaps he should have, at his work, testing his characters' attempts to baffle detectives, whose efforts to solve a crime were equally intelligent and resourceful. For Grayson a nom de plume was unnecessary: he believed the name with which he had been christened – Grayson Montgomery – was suitably genuine, memorable and dynamic, and worthy of his books.

The only disadvantage of selecting Nicholls & Brent (and this was a common failing in agents as well as publishers) was the requirement for a relatively short synopsis which would determine whether the publisher's reader felt the full novel worthy of his firm's notice. Grayson would avoid that hurdle; how could a synopsis communicate the value of *his* work?

Each day Grayson furthered his knowledge in order to plan his fictional crimes. Poison was an obvious weapon; nothing as crude as a firearm or knife would be involved. Grayson was surprised that it was believed that no lethal poisons were to be found in the United Kingdom research establishments. How could this country have identified and treated the victims of otherwise unknown poisons unless they were known by, and possessed by, his laboratory? Grayson would use nothing as the poison of choice in his novel that would be obvious to the police or security services. The secrecy observed by his establishment ensured that several of the potential agents which could be used in his book would be unknown to either.

Meanwhile Grayson rose early to write and spent the evenings after work walking around the streets observing, or sometimes just thinking. The plot would involve much more than the crime. There was the reason the crime was necessary, and the atmosphere the author would create around the hovels and mansions in which it was set.

Each day's writing was typed, printed and proof-read besides being improved at this reading stage. Communications with his family, his colleagues and the authorities improved his work. Until, finally, the book was written. The temptation to call it *The Perfect Crime* was soon dismissed as unworthy of his work and anyway had been used before. *The Unique Crime* would be an accurate description but was similarly dismissed. To reflect the well-rounded nature of its content, Grayson finally settled on *Nothing Is Impossible*. One final typing and reading of the entire work left him satisfied that it was ready for Nicholls & Brent.

Grayson used a file transfer website to send his book to the publisher. He then carefully worded his email informing his prospective publisher of the work that would revolutionise their sales programme.

Following the automatic message, indicating that a full reply would be sent within five working days, he waited confidently but, given his previous experience, with some nervousness, for the publisher's response.

Even the communication stating that complete novels were not accepted from unpublished authors did not deter him. He half expected it. And he planned a visit to the headquarters of Nicholls & Brent.

The size and grandeur of the publisher's offices impressed him without over-awing him. He was careful not to present himself as an aspiring author – he imagined the company's visitors included too many of these and that they would receive a cool welcome. And his politeness and demeanour served as a passport to the grand offices of Mr Brent himself – a grandson of the co-founder of the company.

He waited in an outer office for a considerable time – but he had expected to do so. Finally he found himself in the august presence of Mr Brent – and accepted his apology for the delay with suitable grace.

His case presented, Mr Brent professed that he could not remember which reader had dealt with Grayson's book. But Grayson knew that no 'reader' had dealt with it, that some underling had dismissed it since its writer had not observed the required protocol.

So, he presented the case for his novel and proffered another copy on what he believed was commonly known as a 'memory' stick. Mr Brent, impressed in spite of himself by the case presented, accepted it and promised to give it his attention. Grayson left the building confident that he would.

And the speed with which his novel returned was a vindication of the publisher's promise. So, too, was the detailed assessment of the novel, showing that it had been carefully considered. But the accompanying letter, indicating that Nicholls and Brent would not be publishing it, was a blow that, given the apparently detailed analysis of his work, could not be understood by its author. Had Mr Brent criticised his style, or the structure of the work, Grayson could have understood, even if he would not have remotely agreed. What left him so angry was that the reason for rejection had been 'a lack of realism: the characters were plausible; the method and procedures used in committing the crime were not'.

The day, which had started sunny, had turned to rain and the black skies were in keeping with his darkening mood. He read the letter again, casting the assessment aside. The method of the crime in his book had been tested with infinite patience; the procedures carried out time and time again. Of course no murder had actually been committed as a result but...

While no murder had actually taken place, Grayson himself could have committed that crime undetected. He listened to the rain slapping against the windows and watched rivers appearing on the window panes. It did nothing to lift his spirits but nothing ever would. So carefully had he planned; so diligently had he plotted the victim's downfall that this most unjustified of rejections would blight his life. Successful he might have been in his work – and in other spheres – but his life was meaningless now that his greatest novel had been cast aside.

Despair and fury possessed him. Common sense dictated that he did not act immediately, that he should await morning to consider his path. But he awoke with a similar feeling of anger and plotted revenge: retribution on the man who had failed to understand his genius. Had Brent spent the hours Grayson had spent testing, and re-testing, studying and working on practical demonstrations of his theories?

He had planned his actions and had visited the offices of Nicholls and Brent each day, having taken a period of annual leave to do it. But a suitable occasion had not presented itself. Finally he had awoken to a grey morning, most suited to his mood and purpose. He rose and dressed as if it were any other day – he was a determined man and not to be deterred. He made his way, again, to the Nicholls & Brent building and waited as before in the alleyway opposite the staff entrance.

For the first time Brent appeared to be moving towards the alleyways; to the one parallel to that in which Grayson was waiting. The publisher's intentions were immaterial; his destination unknown - but then he would never reach it. For once, and there had been so many recent frustrations, Brent appeared to be playing into Grayson's hands. Grayson moved slowly but determinedly behind his quarry. He prepared for the attack. Although Brent never saw his pursuer, he would not have recognised him as his erstwhile visitor, as the man whose life had been blighted by his rejection of perhaps the greatest crime novel ever written.

The work of preparation was performed swiftly and without noise; the performance of his act of revenge followed rapidly – Grayson holding his impregnated cloth against Brent's nose. Concerned that the publisher's cry of agony should be heard, he scanned the neighbouring area, but then quickly performed his follow-up tasks: his spraying of the immediate area and his treatment of it with the agent which would ensure that no one else would be identified as the criminal. The place of execution had been well chosen and there was no interruption of these tasks. Brent struggled for breath but his struggle was short-lived. His body relaxed.

The news that Mr Samuel Brent had succumbed to a heart attack appeared on the local news and – his company being such an established one – earned a few column inches in the national press.

Grayson had waited for six months, convinced that he would hear nothing more about it – and he did not. He was gratified by the fact that his method, the same as used in his book, had proved successful. He knew that the nerve agent would not be identified, its existence being known only to those who worked at his research laboratory. It was also easy to clear the infected area. Since it had been developed in England, it had been held only to test any attacks using it, not, of course, that any had been made. Grayson believed that his country would never use it in war.

After those six months, Grayson felt vindicated but not satisfied. He had taken risks: he could have been seen; he was known to have visited Samuel Brent and a study of the publisher's records would have brought his book's rejection to light. However in his book, being fiction, he had been able to avoid such risks and his criminal had taken none. Since Grayson had committed his crime and been unable to avoid risk, how much more foolproof was his book's murder? Its realism could not be faulted. However he felt no satisfaction. His success was unknown.

When eventually the police called, he did not deny his crime. He merely asked what had caused the authorities to identify him as the culprit, hoping that no evidence had been found. It had not. The policeman smiled:

'Your business card – Grayson Montgomery, Author – which was sent to us with the name of Mr Samuel Brent on its back.'

Grayson smiled too, thinking of the long hours during which he would now be able to write – and, as a successful criminal, be believed. His work, he thought, would eventually be published.

The Barrow Cemetery

The dry footpath wound its way up the hill, just as it had in pre-historic times. No doubt those living then would have offered up a prayer for rain to whichever god they favoured, so that their crops would grow on the cracking ground and the parched earth would become green again.

Maddie felt herself a kindred spirit of those farmers who had tilled the land and eked out an existence from this poor soil. And she showed considerable interest in their remains, which she hoped would be coming to life under the careful hands of the archaeologists at the top of the wandering path. Her worry was that the ground was so hard, that digging was difficult and that damage might have resulted from the use of excavating machines moving the upper layers of soil.

Maddie and her team had moved in when the excavators left the site to concentrate on more mundane work. Her challenge was to locate anything which the eighteenth century barrow diggers had left in their desperate bid to open as many of these graves as they could – often seeking to create a record number of 'openings' in a day. These 'diggers' (Maddie would not glorify them with the name of archaeologists) had dug without making adequate – or often any – records of their finds.

The mound (as far as it could be so described) in which Maddie was most interested was almost flat but dipped in the middle. She believed (a belief which was later endorsed by the *Regional Archaeology* of the area) that this was a pond barrow, with – as she had described to her husband Gerald – a circular bank around its perimeter and a curved depression within. His response was that it could have been an ordinary barrow that had simply sunk in the middle. In specifying a bell or bowl barrow to which this indignity may have occurred, he was using knowledge he had acquired from her. Indeed he suggested that this could have been the result of the work of the barrow diggers who were known to have worked on this site. To Maddie's husband, barrows were – as he described them – 'lumps and bumps in the ground'. He could not tell, he admitted, the difference between barrows and what Ordnance Survey maps called tumuli. And he was not sufficiently interested to discover that there was none – except that 'tumulus' could describe any number of types of ancient graves.

At the time that Maddie had embarked upon her work, he was climbing the hill which she had recently ascended, not to monitor her progress but to deliver her lunch – which they ate in the searing sun overlooking the earthworks.

'What have you found?' he asked, without showing any great interest.

'Nothing much,'

'So what have you actually found?'

Maddie, he felt, needed to more accurately describe 'nothing much', suspecting that this represented tin cans, coins – of no age, Victorian or modern pottery and a host of modern 'artefacts' probably left by picnickers on the site.

'So nothing relevant?'

Maddie sighed: 'Not yet.'

'Ah, I thought not.'

'Gerald,' Maddie address her husband, 'there often aren't as you know. There may be nothing at all or it may be of the wrong period or...'

A cry from a trench alerted Maddie to a small find.

Maddie rushed to where a student was holding up a brooch. She took the find and walked back over to Gerald.

'A brooch.'

Gerald smiled: 'A child's brooch; I would say twenty first

century. In fact I have a feeling I've seen them in the shops.'

Maddie grinned and, then, in unison, they burst into uncontrollable laughter.

For all the difficulties it created, the dry spell in a hot summer had given them many opportunities to sit in the sun. They did so now, guiltily looking back at the finder of the brooch who correctly divined that the laughter was occasioned by her find and, incorrectly, that it showed derision of her efforts.

Maddie and Gerald could laugh because 'amateur' archaeology had provided a release for Maddie after her acrimonious redundancy, and relief for her husband from her depression and black moods which had resulted from it. He, nevertheless, could not help being amused by the discovery of so few artefacts of any importance. Despite the affiliation of the local enthusiasts' group to a university body consisting mainly of professionals who designated digs and often allocated one of their number to supervise, it was a source of frustration that Maddie's group was allocated minor digs or ones of which there was little chance of making a major find. The present 'graveyard' was a case in point – where the local parson had written that he had 'dug fifteen barrows in a day and made many finds'. The methods of his excavations were unstated (but assumed to be crude) and his finds unrecorded. The belief amongst the university's archaeological elite was that this excavator had taken what he had pillaged to decorate his home and that his relics had been lost to later generations.

As the dig progressed, this conclusion was being drawn also by Maddie's group and, while they looked to Maddie as a senior amongst them, they were aware that the university had not designated a professional supervisor for the first time – a sign that this excavation was unlikely to be of particular value.

However, the team – with one exception – was enjoying its day out in the sun – a day which contrasted with so many spent in pouring rain, where cleared areas collapsed under the weight of mud which stuck to their trowels, their boots, and increased as the rain continued to fall.

Gerald awoke suddenly, looking up at a cloudless sky and looked over to where Maddie had resumed her work, having first made her peace with the disconsolate finder of the modern brooch.

But, considering the weather and the amiable company of her husband, Maddie's mood began to change. She felt that there was – a dreaded word to serious archaeologists – a 'feeling' about the place. Occasional small pieces of bone were being found and, although very small, they suggested considerable disturbance at the location.

They could, of course, have been animal bone – even modern animal bone – but they were bagged, marked and made ready for the university's laboratory to assess them.

And, then, Maddie took an intake of breath, using her pointing trowel to expose the top of a piece of bone. Could the university have expected a human skull? There could be no confusion, here, with animal bones. Maddie knew that, if genuine finds were expected, the university would have, not only sent a senior professional, but also various types of geo-physical equipment, like the resistivity meters and magnetometers which she knew they possessed. Certainly the initial layer-removal would not have been done by an excavating vehicle. Instead the university's equipment would have been used to determine whether there were promising signs under the ground.

She walked over to bring another to inspect her find.

Betty was as experienced as Maddie and capable of taking over supervisory duties should Maddie be unable to undertake them. She looked where Maddie pointed and descended to her haunches. She looked up at her colleague. She was clearly puzzled.

Maddie looked down and could see – nothing. There, where moments before she had located a skull, there was nothing. Betty nodded to console her companion, but Maddie was inconsolable.

'It was there.'

Betty nodded: 'Yes, I've done that before.'

Maddie looked at her friend and placed her hands on the top of her head, unable to believe that Betty had ever discovered a skull, then been unable to provide evidence of its existence. While she walked away Betty continued to make consolatory noises.

Maddie returned to her scraping with a trowel, then used a heavier tool when she did not locate bone. She looked up to see Gerald standing above her:

'Do you want to go home? The sun, it's too hot. It's affecting us all.'

Maddie angrily denied that her discovery resulted from the effects of the sun.

'Come on, I'll take you home.'

Gerald rolled over and put his arm around Maddie:

'You know,' he said, 'I don't think I've ever heard of anyone who, if asked who was their favourite author, would say: L V Grinsell.'

Maddie smiled: '*Ancient Burial Mounds of England*,' she said, wistfully.

'Just one of the many best sellers.'

Maddie smiled again. He was good at pulling her out of her moods and the hallucination – as she was now beginning to term it - of a human skull was beginning to worry her less. She succumbed to her husband's caresses and sighed:

'You're not a bad old stick.'

She lay for some time, thinking of returning to the site tomorrow with renewed vigour. Then, her obsession with planning for her dig overcame her:

'Damn,' she said, 'I wanted to check the clothes I need for tomorrow; I put all the others in the wash.'

'Now! Oh Maddie, look in the morning.'

'I'll just check,' she said, walking over to a chest of drawers and opening one of its drawers.

Suddenly she stopped, slammed the drawer shut and fell backwards onto the bed.

Gerald rushed to her, holding her with one hand while surreptitiously opening the drawer with his other hand. Maddie's 'digging' clothes were there; nothing else.

'Maddie, did you see that skull?'

She nodded and he carried her back to bed.

He knew better than to jest; he was beginning to believe in that skull.

'Maddie, was it the same skull?'

'They all look alike,' she said tersely, 'but it was a skull.'

Gerald took her in his arms.

'Maddie, there's nothing in that drawer.'

She stumbled out of bed, opened the drawer, and pulled him towards it. He gently pulled her back, knowing that, this time, she had seen nothing other than clothes in the drawer. No skull.

'Am I going mad?'

Gerald smiled: 'I don't know what is happening to you. Do you think it would be better if you didn't go tomorrow?'

'No, I don't think that. I… well, maybe it might be better just to have a rest from it for one day.'

'You've been working too hard.'

He smiled at her again and got into bed, pulling her to him:

'A good sleep will do you good.'

But, after Gerald had fallen asleep, he was not aware of her rising, did not feel the jolt of her body – or her trancelike walk as she advanced to the door of the bedroom.

She took the track that wound to the top of the hill and to the barrow cemetery, walking as if compelled to do so.

By the time she reached the top, Gerald had discovered her absence and made ground on her. As he reached the summit of the hill, he could see a figure, her white nightgown flowing behind her as it rippled in the gentle breeze.

He waited and approached slowly, hesitant about waking her suddenly if she were sleep walking. But she was not sleep walking. She was fully awake but walking in a direction dictated to her. She approached the barrow. She stopped, looking in horror ahead of her.

Then she screamed.

Gerald, too, was stunned by the sight of a mist before her, a wispy figure issuing from it which he could barely discern. To her it had obviously manifested itself more clearly. The mist approached Maddie and she appeared to dissolve into it. Gerald hurled himself at the mist, grabbing Maddie, relieved that she was unharmed. He pulled her away and struck out at the apparition – if such it was. He felt no resistance to his blows, then felt a pain in his head, and in his body. He could not move. He watched helplessly as Maddie moved away. Then, nothing. Maddie was gone and he felt no more.

Gerald awoke, his head pounding and his mouth dry and parched. His first thought was for Maddie. He looked around without seeing her; he scrabbled at the earth, trying to rise but feeling pain in every part of his body. He tried to ignore his discomfort and rose, searching all round the barrow. But he could not find her.

Was it possible that she had returned home? Would she leave him? Was she even aware that he had been there?

Gerald began, painfully, to descend the hill and stumbled to his garden, making as much haste as he could to open the door. He mounted the stairs and opened the bedroom door. The hoped for sight of Maddie lying in bed did not greet his eyes. Only the sheets, flung off the bed as she had left them on her departure. He wanted to search but where was he to go? In an absurd moment, he opened the drawer in which she had seen the skull. The drawer was empty. There was no skull and there were no clothes.

He descended the stairs and began to search the garden and then again climbed the winding path to the top of the hill. The approaching dawn afforded him a clearer sight of the barrows – and the one into which Maddie had seemed to disappear. No one was there; no sprite haunted the hill and Maddie was not to be seen. He sank to the ground; softly he began to cry. Where was Maddie?

'Maddie', he cried, 'Maddie.' But no reply came, and the disturbed surface of the barrow gave no clue as the mist of morning obscured all but the immediate surroundings.

The air was filled with a clammy, clinging atmosphere. Maddie could feel herself descending into damp earth – so different from the conditions with which the archaeologists had been faced in their dig.

She felt a tightness around her as she was sucked down into the barrow, the earth closing up around and above her. All that could be seen ahead was a gaunt frame – a body of such horrific appearance that Maddie tried to scream – but no sound came. She was incarcerated in a tunnel perhaps twelve feet long, her feet almost touching the head that preceded and drew her to it.

Suddenly the space widened, the earth still closing in on top of her as the figure ahead began to lie down.

Had Maddie been capable of coherent thought, she might have remembered that the cemetery had been created in the Bronze Age and that there was a mix of cremation and inhumation, but that the form of burial for this grave had not been determined since the Rev Bardsley's desecration of the site. But, of course, she was not.

Her mind did not function; she was possessed by that of the figure ahead, who had lain in a rectangular receptacle. He fiercely stared at Maddie and motioned to her. She began to lie in an adjacent space, and was somehow aware of where they were; she knew that she would, in future, know where this burial was located.

Next to her, the figure seemed to moderate the hateful stare he had directed towards her. How she read this as a request (not a demand) for reparation for the indignity this man had suffered, she did not know, but there was no doubt of it. She was being entrusted with a mission.

Then the world changed. It was as if she were pushing upwards, her body seemingly detached, until it materialised in the morning light of the site of excavation.

It was there that Gerald saw her, her nightdress soaking, her face pale and her body shaking. She sank into his arms and felt no more.

Gerald needed no more evidence than her wet body to convince him that, at a site parched by weeks of strong sun, she had not been standing there long. His long wait, as he paced the site without seeing her, and then her appearance as one emerging from the earth, convinced him that her story of the skull was no dream, that her experience was not the result of a fevered imagination. He would do everything he could to help her – to banish the demons - if such they were – that possessed her.

But he was surprised that her efforts became concentrated on finding the erstwhile home of that prince of barrow diggers – that record holder (so he had claimed) of barrow openings in a day, Rev. Ezekiel Bardsley. Sure that whatever she did was necessary for her future equanimity, he set about, in the coming weeks, researching local records to discover where the parson had lived. Maddie had always been one step ahead; it was almost as if she had known where they would find the dwelling – as if led to it. Together they had been led to a parsonage in a nearby village. It was here that Rev Bardsley had lived out his days and here that they needed – Maddie felt compelled – to search.

Gerald's first concern – that the occupier of the parsonage would be unwilling to allow them to search it – did not materialise. Indeed the person who answered the door was an elderly, frail man who appeared to accept their claim that they were fascinated by Bardsley's story and would like to see where he had lived. And he offered them every assistance.

Surprisingly their search was quickly completed. In the basement they found what Maddie, but not Gerald, had been expecting – a pile of Bronze Age artefacts – pottery, a dagger, a bracelet, axe heads and… deposited in the corner a jumble of human bones.

It was this to which Maddie was drawn, at first ignoring the other finds. She knew that this mass of bones had been taken from the pond barrow which had occupied so much of her recent time. Why she should have believed that, Gerald was unsure. Maddie knew. She had been guided to them.

And her task was to return them to the place where, although she was hardly conscious of it at the time, she knew she had been led. She would return the grave goods in an exercise which would amaze the artefact-deprived archaeologists and helpers with whom she worked. But she knew she would have assistance – and guidance – as she had had since the first 'finding' of the skull.

She looked to the present occupier of the house:

'Ezekiel Bardsley was a great man,' he said, 'a pioneer in the field of archaeology. And I'm proud to claim him as my seven times great grandfather. I even tracked this place down to buy it to be able to live in his house. These are the finds from just one barrow, but it was a special barrow.'

Despite her profound disagreement with this portrayal of his ancestor, Maddie was anxious to hear more details about the pond barrow she had re-opened.

'It was a warrior chieftain's grave,' Bardsley's seven times great grandson continued. 'And it was his biggest achievement. He left a diary about all his 'openings' and the description of this one was the most detailed. The grave goods showed that the man buried was of high status – there were so many gold implements and body ornaments.'

'But where are they now?' Maddie protested, looking around the cellar.

'Oh, Ezekiel sold them; they were melted down. Barrow diggers did not get paid like archaeologists do now, but Ezekiel made a good profit out of that barrow: most of the trinkets and utensils – gold, copper and bronze - were sold. Ezekiel,' the man chuckled, 'did well from his barrows and none better than the pond barrow on…'

Maddie's mouth opened wide in shock.

'No different, I imagine,' interposed Gerald, 'from the rest of the barrow diggers – and he did keep a record, even if no one but our friend here has ever seen it.'

The occupier, also named Ezekiel – his family having revered their ancestor and bestowed his name upon every generation, smiled: 'You may see it. Of course you may see it. I am so pleased you have come. Too few do – and I only really come down to the cellar when others show an interest in the artefacts – not that many do. Well, really, hardly any.'

Maddie shuddered, then took out a large sack she had brought for the purpose, starting to deposit the bones in it.

Ezekiel's face lost its congenial aspect and his benevolent attitude was gone. He took up a spear head from the hoard and advanced towards Maddie.

Gerald put up a hand to keep him back – he was, after all, an old man. But his ferocity indicated a strength he did not normally show – or perhaps possess.

Gerald tried to calm him, and Maddie:

'Maddie, it's understandable. These are this man's pride and joy. His forefather…'

Ezekiel continued to advance.

'Maddie, you should have asked him. If I'd known you were going to do this…'

She continued to load the bones into the sack and Ezekiel did not check his progress, his spear head level with her face.

Gerald moved to intercept him, but his intervention was unnecessary.

Suddenly from the – now filled – sack arose an unpleasant odour and a misty form appeared. A force emanated from it which swept the attacker off his feet. Gerald looked on in horror as the spirit advanced upon the now prone form.

Maddie quickly gathered the other grave goods and mounted the steps of the cellar. Gerald looked backwards as he followed her, noting that the misty form no longer dominated its victim, who had returned at least to consciousness if not to his previous vigour.

Gerald followed Maddie to their car, helping to bestow the sacks in its boot.

Urged by the being that seemed to accompany and drive them, Maddie drove where she knew she had to go and, having parked at the bottom of the hill, she and Gerald took the winding footpath up the hill:

'He will guide us and give us strength to do it,' she said, as they moved towards the pond barrow of the cemetery.

She Will Survive

She greeted the day; the sun was welcome after hours in the 'school-room' as she termed the dark confines of the hall in which courses where held. Perhaps the training rooms, remote from her place of work, were a little more amenable than her normal workplace, but not by much. And now she had to go back to the normal grind, carrying with her the knowledge she had absorbed in several days of training. She took out her key and pressed the button which would open the car. For a few moments she enjoyed her freedom before facing the necessity of returning to work. But return she must. She made her way through the car park, opening the car door and slipping into the driver's seat.

She was young but she was making her way in a world where being a woman was not easy, in a profession which had long regarded women as less able to cope with its pressures. She may be a woman in a man's world, but *she* could act like a man – better than a man – in stressful situations.

She settled back, pressed the starter button. All appeared normal but she was not happy. She had an odd feeling that all was not right, that somehow there was another presence in the car. A furtive movement. She looked in the rear view mirror but saw nothing. It was absurd that she could have this fear when there was nothing to prompt it. Absolutely nothing.

She knew there could really be no sound behind her seat. She smiled and pressed the accelerator. She felt a slight movement – felt it in her back as if someone were moving in the back seats of the car. It was absurd; she was supposed to be a strong woman in a man's world, making her way, showing them… There had been a sound, the slightest sound. She caught her breath. She felt a cold fear. What if there were someone in the car, someone who…?

But, as she drove out of the car park, she pulled herself together. There had been no more sounds or movement: she relaxed.

But she recalled a case she had read about – a man had secreted himself in the back of a woman's car without her knowledge. She could not remember what he had done, attacked her she thought. She was uneasy but there was nothing now, no sounds, no movement. She could not remember why the man had attacked the girl; the obvious reason she assumed. Had she died? Did it matter? But that would not happen to her. It did not happen to ordinary people. But it *had* happened before.

She wondered how anyone could have got into her car. Had there been a delay after she had used the key to open the car and her getting into it? Of course, she thought, remembering: it had re-locked itself after she had first pressed the key fob and needed, when she arrived at the car, to press it again. That would have given someone time.

She felt another stealthy movement.

She listened. But then she heard a stifled cough. A stifled cough – and further stealthy movement.

She forgot the newspaper report in the realisation that, however unlikely, there was someone in the back of the car.

Another cough. No more movement. And, for a few moments, there was no sound either. One thing was certain; there *was* someone and it was a man. No woman coughed like that.

What could she do? There was nothing she could do but stop and scream. Attract attention. But what would he do to her? All that mattered was that she must keep calm. She did not feel calm. How could she feel calm with the presence behind her?

She neither stopped, nor screamed, although she felt panic rising within her. She wanted to go home but, rising above her panic, was the logical thought that this would tell him where she lived.

She did not want him to know where she lived.

She stopped. Then came the sound she had been dreading… his voice. A menacing voice:

'Carry on driving.'

She put the car into gear and said in a voice unlike her own:

'What do you want?'

What a stupid question. She knew what he wanted.

He ignored her question anyway.

The voice came again:

'Keep driving.'

She battled her shaking:

'Where?'

'Straight on,' he said. 'Don't stop.'

She drove on slowly; bile rose into her mouth. She felt like crying but no tears came.

She was dazzled by the sun; mechanically lowered the sun flap.

He reacted to the movement: grabbed her hair.

'Don't move. Just drive.'

She drove.

He had seen her emerging from the building, and seen her taking out her car key. He had a certain pride in the way women feared him and yet were attracted to him. He saw the lights of her car flash in response to her key. It was the work of a moment to get into her car and crouch low in the back seat. He heard her open the car door a few minutes later. She had taken her time. She had a shock awaiting her.

Suddenly he took her arm: 'Keep driving; just keep driving.'

She kept driving; she remembered her reputation for keeping a calm head. She did not feel calm, but she overcame her fear. He spoke again in a rough voice:

'We're going on a nice long drive. To the forest; we'll have a lot of fun. Or I will!'

She kept driving. She kept her head even when he showed her a vicious knife.

'And you will do what I want you to do.'

She looked at him as he leaned over the passenger seat and said:

'You won't hurt me?'

Another stupid question.

'I might not,' he said. 'You never know. It depends.'

'On what?'

'On how co-operative you are,' he said, holding up the knife.

She instinctively moved away from the knife.

She drove more slowly, quickening at his urging. Suddenly she lurched to the side, swerved and turned down a side street.

'What the…?' He saw that she had turned into the car park of the police station: the police station where she worked.

'Damn you,' he said, falling to the floor of the car, reaching for the knife he had dropped. She was too quick for him. 'I know,' she said. 'Now I know.'

She was quicker than him at every turn. She dived out of the car, locking it with the key that she had surreptitiously manoeuvred into her hand. She could see him getting up onto the seat. Helplessly he looked out of the car as she ran to the desk in the police station and quickly returned with her colleague, the desk sergeant. While she smiled with satisfaction, the sergeant opened the car door:

'Well you did well there; the course is certainly doing you good.'

He looked at her 'abductor': 'She did well. Oh we'll need you for another job this afternoon.'

The 'abductor' smiled: 'Well I certainly hope the next one isn't as smart as this lady.'

When the Devil Drives

The darkness was deafening: a converging sense of the end. The end of everything. I picked my way along the shelves, unaware of what I should find. At intervals a humming sound would assail my ears – before silence, even more dreadful, would descend again and a shimmer of light would invade the darkness. With the light would come a shape – not human, not recognisable. Then the shape would disappear.

I had to reach the light – the proper light: the light of day. But it would take time if it ever came. I knew it would take time. I had done this so often. But, why did I subject myself to this terror? Because I had to destroy what was tormenting me, tormenting us.

I forged on, ignoring as much as possible the obstacles in my way. And I emerged – emerged into the light. I fell into the arms of Anita and Anita held me, drew me back, out into the sun, into the day which others knew.

I sat beside Anita. My embrace showed my love, my gratitude, my feelings of escape.

How could we escape what was tormenting us? I had tried so often. It was part of us; it was within us. It was a part of our lives, of our being. If we moved, it would follow us.

It had all begun on the day we saw the Devil.

The torment would only end when I could destroy his power.

Half of me believed that, by facing him – by penetrating his inner sanctum - I could weaken his hold. Half of me knew it was futile – that I was facing danger for no practical purpose other than showing Anita that I – as man of the house – was doing all I could.

We sat together, grasping each other for the comfort it gave – I because I had experienced fear such as I had never experienced before that awful day, and Anita because she was unsure if I should emerge safely. Anita tried to persuade me not to face our fears head on. I was determined to do so, however futile it might be.

There are many things which change one's life. Nothing, for us, had been more traumatic than that day when Anita had rushed to me with a look in her eyes I had never before witnessed.

She tried to explain, fighting against the incoherence which garbled her speech. What she had seen was beginning to be clearer to me, but not very clear. Could she actually be saying that she had seen the Devil? That she had spoken to him?

The Devil? What, who, was the Devil? A symbol of darkness: he who fights the kindly influence of Christ and appears in other religions as the epitome of evil? Certainly not a person we would encounter, particularly in our secular lives. So I was not expecting a description of a figure with a pitchfork, throwing unfortunates into eternal flames. Not a man with an evil grin. And neither did I get that description. Anita could not speak with clarity but, strangely, her jumble of incoherent speech created a greater impression of the force of evil she had encountered.

Of course it was absurd. There is no Devil – that is all religious symbolism. But that decline into mythology – even into the world of pre-history - stirred a basic instinct: to protect my woman, my home. I held Anita, piloted her into the tunnel from which she had escaped.

'You must show me.'

'I can't; I can't go there again... I...'

And then it appeared, as if it had been waiting, expecting

me. A vast blackness I had not anticipated. Nothing that could be described. No figure, no horns, no punchbowl. Just a tangible darkness.

No speech was heard. Just an unspoken message – a transference of energy which expressed itself to us. Like unseen sound waves:

'Your child.'

Without speaking to each other, Anita and I both looked at Anita's swelling womb.

'I want your child.'

Anita screamed. No words had actually been spoken but it was clear that we had both understood the same threat.

We would not sacrifice our unborn child as both of us believed we were being urged to do.

Our own thought processes were sufficient to communicate. We would not give up our future child to any force, creature... we would *not*.

There was a laugh. Although we had heard no speech and had not spoken, we were aware of laughter – as the darkness dissipated and the light of day returned.

Anita and I looked at each other. Words were unnecessary. We both understood that we had resisted the demand: our child was safe but we would suffer for that resistance. The laughter had given us a sign of our future, an indication of the will of... the Devil.

In bed that night we tried to rationalise. We attempted to speak of what we had seen, heard, experienced. We tried to pretend it had not happened and, if only one of us had lived through it, that thought might have prevailed. But that had not happened. We had both seen it, heard it and experienced something we could never explain.

Anita tried to go with me to rid ourselves of the evil presence which had invaded our lives. Which had caused our friends to avoid us, our relatives to desert us, our pets to die. Which had withered our world and brought our sanity to the brink.

To face it, to attempt to master it, was not a matter of physically going anywhere, but of setting our minds to enter where we could experience that force again. And I was adamant: Anita would not have that experience if I could help it. My own strength seemed to overcome Anita's, not because I was stronger – I suspected the opposite to be true – but because my primeval urge always predominated.

Time and time again I entered that tunnel into which Anita had first disappeared; time and time again I had experienced the force of our oppressor without being able to destroy, or even resist, it. On every occasion Anita let me go with a look of utter horror, an apprehension that I, too, felt. Sometimes it was involuntary. I could not resist its power: it sucked me in. But sometimes I sought it – made a futile attempt to destroy something which, if I were honest, I believed indestructible. Somehow I tried to convince myself that, because my primordial strength governed which of us could enter the tunnel and fight the Devil, it could also destroy 'his' influence.

I had each time succeeded - not in reducing its power – but in escaping its clutches. If the Devil would not have our child he would not entrap us either. Or so I attempted to believe.

We sought the sun whenever we could although, on occasion, the Devil would destroy its influence and draw me – never Anita – into a darker place. But, even when the sun shone brightly and our spirits began to rise with it, and when the Devil did not call me to him, we were afraid. And the approaching birth of our child made us even more fearful.

Anita and I could rarely be found apart. If this state of our being had any beneficial effect, it had drawn Anita and me together – our close relationship becoming as close, we felt, as any human relationship could be.

The weeks passed and the presence of evil in our lives increased. I fought – my protective feelings towards my wife and child uppermost as I resisted its influence. But I always emerged, trembling but unharmed, Anita there to enfold me in her arms – to hug me, to gather me to herself.

Surely no couple has ever approached an event with more trepidation, has ever approached the birth of a child with as much anxiety – a child so welcome, so wanted by us both. And, when Anita was told of 'complications', our fears increased. But, taking Anita into hospital to prepare for a likely Caesarean section proved to be necessary, although Anita went into labour almost as soon as we arrived.

'We do not allow fathers in for Caesareans,' a member of hospital staff told me.

'But I must.'

'We do not…'

'Yes, allow fathers in. You said. But you do not understand why I need to.'

A doctor sighed: 'Your wife, too, is insisting you are with her. But I cannot permit it.'

I sat by the swing door of the operating theatre. As soon as I was aware of hasty movement, I reacted to that activity by pushing open the door. I did it without causing any of the green-gowned staff to look round.

The baby was there – and moved onto a trolley in an incubator. Anita was unaware of what was happening, having had a full anaesthetic. And suddenly it happened. A wild rush of air – a vast resistance on my part. A fight – but, this time, I could feel another force emanating from the incubator. The rush of air had created a figure. For the first time ever, I had seen a figure – fighting too, above the baby.

Suddenly all went still. The baby opened his eyes. And the figure drifted away. Fighting to the last but its strength diminishing, its shape floating and dying in the air.

I could hear the staff shouting.

'Out; you can see…'

I obeyed. With relief I watched as the trolley was wheeled out.

'There, you did not need to do that; you could have jeopardised the operation. The birth could have…'

I did not listen, just stared at my child. A perfect child. No wrinkles, no flat head or distorted features as I had been led to expect. A perfect child. My tears came easily.

And my child looked at me.

And my fears drained into nothingness. Our resistance to evil had been in his defence. And he had responded. He had delivered us from hell.

Lindsey

The vision illuminated the distant past. The group of well-remembered faces; the sun spilling into the room and the sound of the chiming clock marking a distant hour. Each occupant of the reference library had his – or her – head bowed, their work in front of them. Occasionally one would lean back, stretch and look around the room before returning to studies which would equip them for the working life ahead. A life upon which Vincent had embarked, his first post being in the library in which he had so recently worked as a student. As the morning wore on, more heads went back, more arms were raised to ease the stiffness of sitting. All found such relief – all except Lindsey.

It was Lindsey, however, who attracted Vincent's attention. A recent photograph had been taken and had captured the students but, to Vincent, most particularly Lindsey. It showed her looking down at her work with dark eyes, auburn hair cascading down and hiding all but a small portion of her face.

Looking back, Vincent found it difficult to remember her face, so significant was that picture, so arresting the image of Lindsey at work. He could remember that her face had been beautiful although it was the image that was captured in that photograph which was the one that had become seared on his brain.

Having been so recently one of their number, Vincent could vividly recall his feelings then – he had been aware of Lindsey's role in the group. She was part of it; you could not have excluded her.

But she took no part in its social activities, in its 'life' outside study.

She was not unattractive to the male members of the group, and Vincent was convinced that the picture had been taken, by a member of staff, because of her presence in it on that day. He could not have spoken for the others but he was sure that they, like he, were enamoured of that figure who shared their studies.

And Vincent, after all these years, thought of her still. No other person outside his family appeared before him so often – in his dreams, in his musings and when his thoughts should have been elsewhere.

The times he had 'known' Lindsey were golden times, when he would listen to sad songs on his auto-change record player and think of her, as if she were a lost love. She had never been 'his' love any more than she had been paired with any other member of the group. He had no way of knowing but he was convinced that, if approached to 'go out', she would have smiled beautifully and sadly shaken her head. Not that he had ever done so. When the opportunity arose his courage had always failed him; perhaps his colleagues had experienced a similar loss of nerve. Because Lindsey was just beyond reach. Unattainable and untouchable: on a different plain. There were girls – and there was Lindsey.

If he could no longer describe her face, if ever he could, he had always believed it fascinating. Even he felt it absurd that Lindsey was the only girl he had ever truly loved. How else could her enduring memory be explained?

He could not explain either why such a memory had developed into an obsession which blotted out so much of his recent – admittedly mundane – existence, why it had returned with such force. Was it a trick of communication in this wireless age – or a strange contact with a parallel universe? He had never believed in such things, in the past running concurrently with the present or in the ability to recreate the past.

But whatever force was acting upon him; whatever was bringing back more vividly than ever a scene from over fifty years ago, he could not escape it. Sometimes it was not a pleasant sensation, as if an external source were dragging him through an invisible wall. Until…

He sank before the lowering sky, his head hurting with its over-powering darkness. Rain threatened but never came; instead the stormy sky seemed to seep into the oppressive stillness. He started to move forward, feeling an impulse which was driving him ever further into the past. Then the clouds cleared. He felt a surge of relief but was still in the grip of that external source. Visions appeared before him. He sat in a known place as if its very familiarity would bring comfort. It brought neither comfort nor pain. He continued to sit – and viewed this world from the outside. This was his world but he felt remote from it. He was in the gardens, in the building. Was he a sprite? What sort of observer was it that seemed to have no being, no solidity?

And then she was there before him.

In a period he remembered, but not a specific time.

And he was in her life, keenly aware of her actions, knowing that Lindsey had… He held his head. What was happening to him? He slumped back on the seat.

Lindsey took her books and carried them out to the lily pond in front of the library. The sun reflecting on its water made patterns on the foliage. Lindsey drew out her work and laid aside her case.

She had been working for some time before she put away her pen and her books. She was about to leave the gardens but stood for a moment, indecisive. Then she seemed to come to a decision. She hoisted her bag on her back and mounted the steps back into the library and up the stairs to the reference library. It was almost empty, most of the students having left for lunch. With a moment of courage, she approached the woman at the desk.

Was the reference librarian still here?

A woman wearing thick glasses went into a back room and returned with an elderly man. Lindsey was unsure what to do. He was not the person she wished to see, but he smiled kindly at her request.

'Ah!' the woman in the thick glasses said, realising the girl's mistake: 'the person you want is *not* the reference librarian.'

The man who bore that title, who had immediately realised who Lindsey sought, smiled:

'I'm sorry, you've just missed Vincent; he's gone to lunch and he'll be at another library this afternoon.'

'I wanted to see him about a book he got out for me,' she said untruthfully.

'I can get it for you,' said the woman in glasses.

The reference librarian smiled again and, ignoring the helpfulness of his colleague, and with a better understanding of Lindsey's request, said:

'I'm afraid he won't be here for a little while – he's going on leave. But you could see him this afternoon,' and told her of the library in which he would be working.

Lindsey tried, without success, to locate him that afternoon. And, in a succession of visits to the main reference library, was unable ever to find him. Her success came on a day when the wind was wild – it blew directly into her face and affected her spirits. She put her wet outer clothes on the clothes rack and settled uncomfortably at the table. He came out of the back room. She looked towards him and noticed that he had looked her way. Since he then studied the work before him, she too looked down, and made to rise. Then she sat back down. He would not want to see her.

It was not long after this occasion that she was informed that he had moved to take another post.

Since the rain had ceased and the wind had eased, she descended to the library gardens and sat by the pond. She was determined: she would not cry. But perhaps she did. It was difficult for Vincent to see.

During this time, Vincent had followed her life, been part of it and experienced her thoughts. He was not sure if he were inventing a story that realised his dreams, but he did not think so.

He looked up at the, now blue, sky and the face of Lindsey looked shyly down upon him. She appeared to his right. To his left... she was everywhere he looked. He gazed at her beautiful face – exactly as he had seen it all those years ago. And then, to his consternation, it began to fade.

His head had ceased to hurt; his eyes were raised to the sky. The sun flooded the area around. He looked for her – and there, just before him, he could see her long hair, her dark eyes. So real, but fading. That face must not disappear. He cried out: 'Don't go; please don't go.'

But the vision before him was fading. He pleaded; he tried to follow but there was nowhere to go.

Pleading would not help; he followed her features as they dimmed. He stood for some time after they had faded into nothing. 'Lindsey!' he cried; 'Lindsey!'

The garden was empty; Lindsey was gone and no one from his mundane world had had the effrontery to replace her. The world was older; the impression of an outsider was gone. He was a part of the modern world, of a place he did not wish to inhabit, without joy or magic. He walked, unsure of his progress, looked at the building ahead but did not see it. He was staring at nothing. He turned to go, trying to hide the tears in his eyes.

He never saw her again.

The Secret of Meredith Ladeley

My name is Meredith Ladeley and I have a secret. But I am letting you into my secret.

I can see into the future.

I don't have a time machine or anything like that and I can't foretell world events. It's just that, when I feel deeply about something, I can often get a flash of how things are going to turn out.

Take my father for instance; I have to confess I was never close to him, but blood is thicker than water as they say and I did have respect, and some affection for him. He brought me up single-handedly, he… Well, enough of that, my father's death was the first time I had seen into the future. You can say, well, he wasn't young; no he wasn't. And perhaps most people could have forecast the end of his life. But not the very day. And not in the way it happened. Sadly it wasn't something I could prevent – or I would have done so. I couldn't stop it happening because everything I see eventually happens. I can't stop it.

It can be a curse – like when our friends, Maisy and Philip's marriage broke up. I was quite fond of old Philip, but I couldn't condone what he did. Seeing the girl he went off with, I could see the temptation, but we are all tempted aren't we? In some way.

Well, Philip came crying back to Maisy when his 'new love' moved on to some other poor sap. Some of our friends blamed Maisy, said she was being harsh. But she wasn't. I was right behind her – because I knew all about it.

I can't say I always see everything – I rarely do. I see flashes as I've said. And it's only like a clip from a film. I could see Maisie and I could see Philip, and I could see a brief glimpse of the day she threw him out. But then that's all that was needed; you could build up a more or less complete picture from that.

You may ask me why I don't use my 'skill', if that's what it is - 'strange ability' perhaps would better describe it – to my own advantage. Well, it doesn't quite work like that. No, I don't see winning lottery numbers; I don't get an inkling of the rise of a company's fortunes that would encourage me to buy shares. I'm not the sort of person who buys shares anyway. Too risky. But there is one notable example of where I was able to use my talent - yes, that's it, talent - to feather my nest. Or feather *our* nest I should say. My wife Judy has struggled along with me for years and it's been hard for us both. So I thought, well, why not give her a break? And it was presumably because I was so worried about money that I got another of my glimpses of the future.

Again it was a flash: a horse crossing the finishing line and a voice – like a commentator's voice – saying: 'Never Too Late, now that's a surprise. He's never shown that form before'.

Now, as I've said, I'm not one who takes a risk. I don't buy lottery tickets and I've certainly never bet on a horse. I only buy my golf club's lottery tickets because I might appear mean if I don't. And, as for knowing about betting on the horses, I didn't know where to start. But I did know that a horse producing a surprising result was a good animal to put some money on. So I went to a book-maker's and asked how I went about it. I didn't want to let anyone else into my secret. I didn't know the date of the race but I soon found that out, and I'd remembered the name of the horse. So I fed the man in the betting shop with that information and he advised me how I should put my bet on. Now, I played it cannily. I knew that, if a horse won that wasn't expected to, there might be an 'enquiry'. There might be bad things that had caused it, 'nobbling' of other horses, doping – well, you know the sort of things – most of us have read Dick Francis books!

So I did not want someone coming back to me and accusing me of being complicit in a doping scandal, so I put money on several other horses too – all of which had low odds and were expected to win. I put quite a lot of money on them too – that would show the bookmaker that, just because I was a novice, I wasn't a fool.

Although he did raise his eyebrows when I came round to putting a substantial sum – oh, let's be honest, all my savings - on Never Too Late in the Riverhead Stakes. But he put the money on for me. He didn't tell me that the horse was a no-hoper. He was expecting to make a killing. Serve him right. And the irony was that three of the other six horses I'd put money on won too! That wasn't really supposed to happen but no one came knocking on my door – so there was obviously no enquiry or, at least, if there was it didn't find anything untoward. And Never Too Late started a run of results that showed that he wasn't such a no-hoper after all.

The reason I took advantage that time was because we were very low on money – those savings were being kept for a rainy day and – remember how careful I am – they weren't going to be spent unless we were absolutely desperate. If you knew what we lived on, you'd think it had been raining for months!

And why were we on our uppers? We – or at least Larry Wainwright and I – had a successful business. But I never seemed to see much in the way of the proceeds. Larry was doing alright; I didn't understand it. You can say I was naïve – I was, and still am naïve – yes, I admit it. I realised *that* when I looked into the matter and discovered just how much he was squirrelling away without letting me into *his* secret.

I had thought he had dipped into his savings – and I knew the extent of mine, made in the pre-Larry days when Judy and I were running a similar business. Now, I knew differently and regretted believing Larry's stories about how throwing in my lot with him would increase my profits. He was careful not to promise me the earth. Probably because he knew what I was like – and because he was already planning to swindle me. He put the reduced income down to temporary bad luck. But it turned out to be bad luck for him too.

Now, I've never been a violent person – definitely not. And the thought of hitting anyone would have shocked me. I hate violence in others too. So I was surprised at myself – at how I reacted when I discovered what Larry was up to. I knew Larry to be a pretty strong man – but I was stronger. I knew that. So I was careful not to do anything I'd regret. But then, well I just snapped. Suddenly I hated him as I'd never hated anyone. I should have called somebody after I'd left him on the floor – but I didn't dare.

And the worst thing happened. I had one of my flashes of the future – and there was a doctor proclaiming Larry to be dead. I had another later, with a body being loaded into a meat wagon on a trolley, with police cars around.

It won't surprise you to know that this took its toll. I became morose; Judy couldn't understand it. But it became so bad that I felt I had to explain it. I said I'd killed someone. She was shocked – well, she would be wouldn't she? She wanted to know all about it, who I'd killed and why. Eventually I told her it was Larry and she laughed. Laughed. I was staggered. How could she laugh? Well, I soon discovered why when she said she'd seen him at the supermarket. He had a black eye, she said, and he wasn't looking too bright, but, otherwise, well, he was definitely alive. Buying beer for a party apparently. Or that's what he told Judy.

I couldn't understand it; my glimpses of the future had never been wrong before. Perhaps, just this time… thank goodness. Never Too Late winning the Riverhead Stakes hadn't been wrong. Anyway believing that my premonitions could be wrong on occasion didn't somehow satisfy me. I was so convinced that they were always right that I began to think there was more in it. Perhaps Larry had suffered some sort of internal injury and would die later. Perhaps… Oh it was no use speculating – but I couldn't just dismiss it. I had killed Larry and I knew it.

This couldn't have been a good time for Judy. She had had

to suffer lack of money and been as faithful and devoted as any wife could be. She couldn't understand why I was so depressed, though, when all our money worries were behind us. I know she suspected that there had been something suspect about that big win – something I didn't want to tell her. Otherwise why would I be acting like the hero of a Shakespearean tragedy?

Anyway I told you how faithful she had been to me in the bad times. Now, in what she considered to be better times, she couldn't understand why I was paying her less attention and acting like a bear with a sore head. I began to believe, even, that Judy was being unfaithful to me.

I couldn't prove that: Judy was a jolly person and she had lots of friends. I suppose she flirted with some of the men – I didn't mind that. We all flirt sometimes don't we? No, the big problem was that the man she saw most – was Larry. 'I'm popping round to see Larry.' 'I saw Larry at the supermarket.' 'Do you know what Larry said to me?'

And, yet I had told her that Larry had been cheating me. She obviously hadn't believed me although she knew that I had ended our business associations and that I had started a new business without Larry. Although she knew that more money was now coming in – she handled the accounts for the new business after all – she didn't seem to believe that Larry was capable of doing all I told her he had been doing. Obviously not; she wouldn't still pass the time of day with him, let alone go round to his house.

At the time, I kept asking myself – does it matter? After all Larry was going to die. For whatever reason, he would be carted out into the meat wagon. Whether as a result of what I had done to him or not, I couldn't tell.

Judy began to make a life of her own. She would ask if I wanted to go out for a meal, but I never really wanted to. I couldn't somehow disabuse myself of the idea that I was responsible for Larry's future death and that I should pay for it. And she began to go to the theatre with her girlfriends – and not invite me. She'd even go for walks on her own. I couldn't really blame her. I was hardly congenial company.

And, if I were honest, I was responsible for that new independence and there was nothing serious between her and Larry. Eventually that became obvious.

It was when she went round to his house one day – she even told me she was going. I'm sure that she was trying to make me jealous so that I would snap out of it. The trouble was that, innocent as it was to Judy, it wasn't to Larry. I'm not saying that he wanted to take Judy from me – or anything like that. Just that he was different from us. I'd heard about his 'affairs' – that isn't quite the right word for them. Conquests might be, although a conquest usually ends with someone taking over. Larry never did. He just led girls up the garden path. You know what I mean. And that's what he did to Judy. She went round all unsuspecting and Larry reverted to type. That's a strange expression but I can't say this in any other way. He raped her. Perhaps he thought she was willing, but I knew there was no collusion; it would have been obvious to him as soon as he started to move in.

Judy came home in a right state. Her clothes weren't even straightened out. She was crying – well worse than that. She obviously felt terrible. I had to put her to bed. She told me all about how… Oh, I don't want to repeat what she said. I'd rather forget it. I'd rather forget what I did too, how I went round to that bastard's house and…

Not for the first time my superior strength told in our struggle. I didn't think I'd hit him that hard. You know, I told you I wasn't a violent person, and now I'm telling you that, for a second time, I'd knocked a man down.

But I had never done it before and I've certainly never done it since. It was because it was Larry. He somehow made my blood boil. There were occasions, well just two occasions, when he pushed me to a fury that made me lose it with him. I ask you – what would you do if someone raped your wife? You see what I mean?

Well, the day after I'd had the fight with Larry, I got Judy out of bed and promised her I'd try to be a better husband, more cheerful – I wouldn't take her for granted; I'd take her out more – or I'd take her out full stop.

It was easier for me now because I began to see the premonition about Larry was likely to be true. Sometimes I saw the future but, unlike with my father, and Maisy and Philip, I didn't always know exactly when the 'event' would occur. I didn't with the horse race; I'd had to look up the runners for future races to find that out. So my seeing Larry dead was obviously more in the future than I'd imagined. I should have to be more careful about that.

And Judy was feeling better; I had no future worries about Larry, but I wasn't so stupid as to think my troubles were over. That is why, when, a few days later, Judy went to the door, I tried to beat her to it.

Judy stared at the people on the doorstep; perhaps she thought the police were calling because of the rape. Anyway she looked at me, puzzled, when I put my coat on and began to go with them.

'I won't be long, darling,' I said.

It didn't really cover the situation, I know, but I told her that, whatever she heard, everything would come out alright.

And when she came to visit me, I still tried to reassure her. Do you remember that I told you that I was non-violent? (OK, yes, several times). Well I'm not violent unless provoked – but that doesn't really explain it: unless I'm driven to take action. And that's what I'd done with Larry. He was the one with an ungovernable temper and a violent streak. I knew that, with Judy, he'd acted partly out of revenge, and he was expecting my visit to tell him that I shouldn't try it on again with her. It was pointless really on my part. I knew Judy would never go near him again and I knew Larry wouldn't try to. Perhaps I did have an idea that I wanted Larry dead. And, when he came at me with a weapon, I was sufficiently calm to believe that I could use the argument of self-defence. After all, no one knew of the previous occasion I'd knocked him down – come to think of it that, too, would have been in his mind as he came at me.

And they let me go. I knew they would because I'd had another premonition (even before I went round to Larry's). Judy couldn't understand how I could have taken it all so calmly.

Well, that's it really. You've read what no one else knows. I'd be grateful if you returned my letter (sorry but an email would have been too risky) at your convenience.

And never tell anyone about this, please. I am trusting you.

The Girl Who Was Morning

The grass glittered with frost; a haze of mist reached almost to it. The early morning silence accentuated one small sound as the hem of her white dress gathered the gem-like frost as she walked slowly across the field. Her destination was uncertain, her identity unclear. She was seen from the back, her dress plain – redolent of a past age but not out of place in the present one. Her sleeves did not billow in the stillness, nor her long white dress. Her legs could only be imagined and even her face, from the tilt of her head, in its forward motion, was unseen. Her hair, her long red hair was gathered at the back and reached nearly to her waist. She was morning. She was unattainable, untroubled and untouched. She was morning.

And he did not, could not, touch her. She was his morning. She was in the air ahead of him as her image dissolved into the reality of the day. He sat up, sighed and prepared for it – the mundane day. A day at a desk behind the rows of others whose ordinary lives were unalleviated, untroubled by the lady of the morning.

The opening of the mundane working day, however, was always a high point, a meeting with the team: his team. Help with a database issue; assistance with scripting – all he could give. But there was Sandy. Sandy could not have been more different from his perennial mornings' vision. She was blonde – or possibly not as blonde as she appeared. She was short. But she had a lovely face. He could not have imagined her in a long white dress floating over fields of frost. She was not a vision but, combined with her lovely face, was a beautiful nature. As she introduced an issue to the planning meeting, it was entered on the computer and became the basis of a project. She, like the rest of the team, was hard working, diligent – and loyal.

It was a gradual process, the procession of feeling which led him to an awareness that he appreciated her, was fond of her, that he liked her more than other girls he had seen. He passed his working day thinking of her to the extent that he had to be reminded of his next meeting.

He went to the bar and bought their drinks in The Swan. He was very pleased that she had agreed to go to The Swan with him at lunch time. It was summer and she wore a sleeveless dress. He liked her arms, her tapering fingers and the way she took her drink. She smiled. He wondered if he would ask her to come with him for a day out on the Downs – where they could walk. He checked his phone for the weather forecast – on Saturday it would be dry and sunny. She smiled. Yes, she would be pleased to come. He eased back in his chair. She would be pleased to come.

Pulling down the blinds, he turned out the light and put his book down. Saturday, so soon. He felt excited like a young boy in love. Where would they go? Should he decide? Should he ask her where she would like to go on the Downs? Should he… He slept. Slept until the dawn started lightening the room. Then a field appeared to him, a field of frosted morning – and, emerging from his misty mind – the girl. Not the girl who had occupied his day thoughts but the girl of his dreams.

She walked – her white dress clinging to her in the familiar way, the hem of her dress providing the only sounds as it trailed on the grass.

Then, for the first time ever, she turned. She looked straight at him, her face one of unbelievable beauty. And then, in the billows of sleep, she smiled. She smiled at him. He could feel himself smiling back – smiling in his sleep.

Morning came. She was gradually fading and he rubbed his eyes. As he did so, he remembered what had been planned for his meeting on Saturday. The girl who was morning – so lately the sole occupant of his thoughts – disappeared, and the reality of the day banished her. He collected his brief case and prepared to walk to the station. On arrival, the girl who was to be his companion on Saturday smiled a beautiful welcome. It did not compare with that of 'the girl who was morning' but it was a nice smile and it pleased him. He returned it as he settled into his desk.

They met again at The Swan. It was time to discuss when and where on the Downs they would meet – and walk. She asked him to decide. She was used to taking his direction and he made suggestions with which she readily agreed. On parting at The Swan, he gave her a kiss on the cheek – just a brush against her skin but somehow significant in their relationship.

That night he settled down to sleep. He had been asleep for some time, approaching the early hours. It was when she came. She smiled as she had smiled on the previous night but there was something in the smile that troubled him. As morning approached she continued to smile but there was a definite element of disapproval in that smile. All was not well. He called to her but she began to dissolve into his wakefulness. He called more loudly; he pleaded but to no avail. For the first time he regretted her going. As the field passed too, he felt anxious. He prepared for work without any enthusiasm despite the prospect of Sandy and the pleasures that the day promised.

As he entered the room he was greeted with an even greater smile than she had previously given him. Saturday was approaching and Sandy's enthusiasm was clearly growing. He delivered a perfunctory smile. As he sat down he felt guilty, looked up at her still smiling face and gave what he felt was a more appropriate greeting. A more fitting welcome to one whom he was increasingly regarding as 'his girl'.

It was that night that the headaches began. Nothing too worrying. Irritating. But not worrying. He managed to sleep – to see his vision and to regret her passing at the coming of day. The week passed and Saturday came. On Saturday he awoke with a greater headache. It was nothing. He had had headaches before. Everyone had headaches. So he bad farewell to his lady of the morning – reluctantly but, he felt, loyally.

When Sandy and he walked it was not like his dream. She walked with her head against his, her arm around him. This was reality. This was pleasure unshrouded by mist, frost and mystery. His pleasure lasted all day and did not dissolve. They lay on the grass on the hill and surveyed the Downs. He felt that this day had given her the pleasure he had expected to feel himself. And, yes, of course he was pleased. He looked at her sweet face beside his, at her smile, at her hair. And he smiled too.

At night the headaches became worse. Sandy had suggested they meet again on Sunday, at her flat, and he had accepted. He thought he ought to have suggested his own house but did not do so. There was something which held him back. He would not suggest that – and he knew why.

Sunday began with a light rain falling; when the girl of the morning came to him, he had called her, begged her not to leave him. He woke himself by his cry: 'Please don't go; please don't leave me.' But she had. She had faded very quickly.

But Sunday passed pleasantly. They braved the intervals between the showers, walking the streets, their arms comfortably entwined and their slow progress occasionally interrupted with a chaste kiss. Was this his girl? Of course. Of course Sandy was his girl. Back at her flat he could feel the strength of his feelings surface. There was an inevitability about their love making. He stayed the night.

As he surfaced, he noticed that she was looking strangely at him. He conquered the strength of his headache to ask her. What was the matter? He had loved last night. She had loved it too. But she still seemed puzzled:

'You called out.'

'I called out? What did I say?'

'You said: "You have not come. Don't leave me. Please don't leave me".'

He looked down. He did not know he had spoken but – yes – that is what he had felt.

'You should have no fear that I will leave you,' she said. 'We have loved. We are in love. Aren't we?'

'Yes', he said quickly. 'Of course we are.'

Much to his relief the girl of the dawn walked the morning fields on Tuesday morning. Although a relief, he did not feel completely comforted by her reappearance. He had been feeling unwell and he felt worse this morning. His head pounded. No ordinary headache this. And her beautiful face looked at him angrily. No smile. Anger.

Many days passed; many more meetings occurred at work. Lunch time drinks had become the norm. But Sandy was becoming less happy with their arrangements. For she had noticed his abstracted air. He no longer kissed her cheek as they walked along. It was as if he was no longer in love with her.

She asked him. He smiled and dismissed the suggestion. He put hands to his head. He increasingly did this. Was he ill? He was certainly in pain.

There had been a number of days when the girl of the morning's appearance had been fleeting, when the dream had quickly faded. This could not happen. It must not happen. Then one day, the girl of the morning did not appear at all.

He looked forward less to his lunch times at The Swan. The pains increased and his work suffered. His 'love' for Sandy became less strong and they planned no more meetings. He looked at her over his computer. Her face was sad. She caught him looking but it was a sorrowful smile she gave him. Her eyebrows were raised questioningly. He held his head in his hands; the pains were increasing. He made excuses about not meeting at lunch time but he could not bear to see her sadness. He often saw her looking at him but, unable to face her,. pretended not to notice.

When she applied for a transfer, he granted it.

That night he went home desperately worried. He slept but the pain had ceased. The morning was approaching and the grass glittered with frost, a haze of mist surrounding it. And the early morning silence accentuated the one small sound. The hem of her white dress gathered the gem-like frost as she slowly walked, her face turned to him, smiling and as beautiful as ever. He sighed as he awoke to a bright morning. There was not a cloud in the sky.

The Riddle of Dack Street

Dominic Beecher was not the world's most organised man; however, he was determined to do this job properly; he would be judged by it and success would achieve Vernon's aim – the most important thing Dominic had ever wanted.

So he studied his gun.

Or, well, Vernon's gun. Dominic admitted that he knew little about guns, but, with greater honesty, he would have admitted to no knowledge at all. It was Vernon who knew about guns. And that was enough for Dominic.

It was in planning, and organisation, that he needed to shine in this matter. And, again, less than honest in his assessment of his own qualities, he felt that his strengths lay in these areas and that, therefore, he would succeed in achieving the allotted task.

In order to undertake it, he required the name and address of his victim, the man Vernon wanted killed. He was hardened to contemplation of the act itself. The name had been supplied by Vernon – E. Smith. He had even, helpfully, expanded the 'E' to Edwin. A common surname so there must be no mistakes. The address, he had been informed, was Dinton Gardens. Not a road he knew but this was no problem. There were such things as maps! To find the number of the house in Dinton Gardens was his next task.

And, fortunately for Dominic, E Smith (or E R F Smith as he was listed) was one of those, seldom found in these times, whose name and address appeared in the telephone directory. This was not the only location information he found for the unfortunate Edwin Smith. Post code finder supplied more – and Dominic was able to insert this in his car sat. nav. in order to make his initial investigation of the property.

And there it was, number 12 Dinton Gardens, a 1950s dwelling next to a new property which was surrounded by a garden which was unfenced and undeveloped – and that left what Dominic had begun to regard as the 'target house' more exposed.

He had no worries about E Smith's prospective demise; nor did he have qualms about seeing his 'victim' in person. What he saw when he *did* see him was a perfectly normal looking man: tall and fair haired, with a stately build and muscular frame. Were his task to kill him by physical attack, he would not have viewed the prospect with the same equanimity that he showed, knowing that the gun would do the work remotely.

And here he made his first mistake; Mr Smith noticed him and smiled a friendly 'Good morning'.

Again, it mattered not to Dominic that this was his quarry – and that the man whose destruction he was planning seemed to be a very pleasant person. Plenty of pleasant people faced sudden ends. And Vernon would have good reason for this murder; perhaps Edwin Smith was not as pleasant a person as he had appeared. He had complete faith in Vernon. What worried Dominic was that he was now known to his potential victim. He would not inform Vernon of this mistake – well, not, at any rate, until after his job had been completed.

And, Dominic's was not a face that people remembered; he did not live near Dinton Gardens and was therefore not likely to be recognised as he went about his normal business – as long as he did not reveal himself during future, inevitable, visits to Smith's house.

His next task was to investigate the house's layout and the potential for a gunman to approach the occupant without being seen. So, on his next visit, he kept watch on his 'target' from the cover of a large bush. The man entered the house and Dominic left his hiding place. He did not have his gun with him; there was much else to do before, what he had begun to regard as 'the act', was undertaken.

There was a path which circuited the house; the neighbouring property had no fencing so he could approach number 12 closely, being careful to avoid the rubble with which its garden was strewn. Dominic was able to check each window as he passed it and discovered that the lounge and the kitchen abutted the path. This part of the job would be easy. If undertaken during the day, the house's occupant was unlikely to be in the upstairs bedrooms for long periods.

And this led Dominic to his next task. Was Mr Smith now, he considered, the sole occupant of the house? Was there a Mrs Smith? Or even, heaven preserve us, miss or master Smiths?

After a week of visits, during which he was careful to remain unseen, he had a clear picture of what he believed to be Mr Smith's routine. He was single, had no partner, and seemed to have few friends, or at least friends who frequently visited him. This he found strange: a man of his attractive appearance had, apparently, no close circle of friends.

But perhaps that was why he had been selected as Vernon's victim – a man whose life had determined his fate – and who had gone through it antagonising his fellow man – and making enemies. Vernon had not even hinted at his reason for desiring his death; he obviously had good reason.

Much of the remainder of the final week before 'the day' was used by Dominic to research into his potential victim's mode of life. When did he leave for work? When did he visit others? When did he make himself vulnerable to the shot which would strike him down?

The day for 'the act' to be accomplished was fast approaching. He did not fear its coming: he had no concern for his victim, having no moral qualms. If Vernon had determined that this man must die, then this man must die, and his death would be completely justified. He also had total belief in, and complete devotion to, Vernon. He did not worry about the inevitable consequences since his faith in Vernon to deal with them was unshakable.

What Dominic feared was that, despite all his planning - and he had never planned for anything as he had prepared for this day – he might not succeed.

It was with this fear that, on a sunny morning, he approached 12 Dinton Gardens. It was as if his confidence was disappearing like the sun which was slipping back behind a cloud – a dark cloud.

After half an hour of walking – he would not leave a vehicle near to the scene of the potential crime – the sun had not made a reappearance: the cloud (and its companions) had taken over the sky and there were even a few drops of rain with which to contend. And those drops became heavier until Dominic was putting up his rain hood and disappearing into the anonymity of his raincoat like a tortoise withdrawing its head into its shell.

He began to look for compensations. His hood would serve to conceal his identity; indeed, he wondered that he had not thought to wear it anyway. Then he considered a mask, or a balaclava. But it was too late for that. And the rain would deter potential witnesses to his crime from leaving the comfort of their homes.

And then, arriving at the house, and crouching behind the hedge, he gasped. In all the weeks of his surveillance and research, no visitor had ever entered this house. But, today, a very attractive female was preparing to do so, having rung the bell.

The occupant answered the door and, soon, the couple were locked in a fond embrace. The door closed. And Dominic was filled with indecision. He felt he must do something. He crept from his place of concealment to the nearest side window, that of the lounge. He peered in, hastily withdrawing at the sight of the couple in a warm embrace. Dominic considered that anyone in the house other than 'his target' would be a hindrance; no, more than a hindrance. He could not contemplate completing his task in such a situation. And, far from the visitor retiring to another part of the house, it looked to Dominic as if she would become inseparable from the house's occupant. Given his lack of skill with a gun, it would not do if the fatal shot were to bring down both. Would Vernon accept a double killing?

Just how far did Vernon's desire for Smith's liquidation extend? Not that far, Dominic thought. In a way that gave him an excuse not to commit the crime on that occasion, when another person in the house was likely to react to the gunshot and start proceedings which would lead to his apprehension.

Dominic retired behind the bush which had become his second home during the past few weeks. Then, when the couple in the house showed no sign of re-appearance, he started on the long walk home. He stopped in one of the refuges which he had discovered were suitable to avoid prying eyes. And it proved useful.

He withdrew his mobile phone, hesitated, then stopped.

Was it wise to use his phone? He had heard that criminals had been tracked by the location of their phones. And he also remembered Vernon having told him he must never use it, must never contact him and should wait for calls. With some relief, he put it away – he had so nearly disobeyed instructions. He had been so close to losing Vernon's confidence.

But his walk home was no happier – because he had failed in his task and had no means of admitting this and of obtaining new instructions. And he had to wait until Vernon's phone call – which would not, he felt, be a congenial one. So, having divested himself of his wet clothing, he sat, his head in his hands, to wait.

'You have not done it!'

'I know, I know,' Dominic yelled. 'Please, Vernon, I could not. I *will* do it – tomorrow. I could not while there was another in the house.'

'Another?'

'Yes, a woman; he…'

'I saw no woman.'

'You *saw*; you mean you were there?'

'Not there but, from where I was hidden, I saw no woman.'

Dominic's depression deepened. Did his presence mean that his friend distrusted his ability? And why had Vernon not witnessed the visitor's entrance if he had been nearby?

Vernon continued: 'But I wasn't that close. There could have been... Yes, I'm sure there could have been a woman.'

If not an apology, the statement satisfied Dominic.

'Tomorrow: you must go tomorrow but, this time, we will assume that a postponement might be necessary. If the woman, or anyone else, appears, that is.'

Dominic breathed a sigh of relief.

'Tomorrow?'

'Tomorrow.'

And 'tomorrow' started as had the previous day but, on this day, the sun did not seek refuge behind a cloud and neither did a cloud, or clouds, invade the sky. Dominic looked up. Predominantly blue, with the sun standing out in all its early morning glory.

Dominic felt heartened as he made his way to 12 Dinton Gardens. Surely today would be the same as every other day during the last week. Would the woman have stayed the night though? Their closeness on the previous day suggested that this might be a strong likelihood.

So he approached the house from his bush with considerable trepidation. How would he tell that she was not in another part of the house, ready to leap into action as soon as the shot was heard? Quite suddenly Dominic developed a determination to finish the job irrespective of the difficulties.

He peered into the kitchen, but it was unoccupied. He moved round to the lounge and, there, sitting at a computer at the far side of the room, was the man whose life he was about to extinguish. He raised the gun and pointed it through an open window. It was almost as if, on this more promising day, everything was going his way.

He lined up the gun, pulled the trigger and fled.

He knew he should not run but he was incapable of performing the task in the measured way Vernon's instructions had recommended.

But it was easy for Vernon to say that; he was not carrying out the crime.

Dominic realised just how much the last few weeks and, particularly, the last few hours had affected him. He had criticised Vernon. Not to his face, perhaps. But that did not matter: how could he even think critically of his only friend?

He banished all such thoughts and settled down in his home, satisfied at last that he had done his job, that he had lived up to Vernon's belief in him. That he was deserving of the praise which would be heaped upon him.

Then the phone rang.

Dominic leapt to answer it.

But there was no praise. There was only anger:

'You have not done it.'

'I have. I have. I have done it. I have killed him. He was dead,' he said without being able to justify that statement. 'I could not have missed,' he blustered, beginning to be unsure of his ground. Had he felt the man's heart? Had he even looked in to determine whether he was lying on the ground? Was it conceivable that, because of the distance across the room, he might have missed?

'You didn't miss; you didn't even go near the house. You didn't even make the attempt.'

'I did. I did. Vernon, I swear I did.'

Dominic was near to tears and, as Vernon continued his tirade, they fell. He held the phone away from his face and then put it back on its rest.

How could he say that? How could he be so….

The phone rang again.

'Dominic; he is not dead.' Vernon's anger, for a moment, had subsided. 'Did you go to Dinton Gardens?'

'Yes, yes.'

'And you saw Smith, Edwin Smith?'

'Yes, and I killed him. I definitely killed him. Or at least I shot him.' Finally, Dominic mumbled: ''Well, I shot at him.'

'You shot at the man at 14 Dinton Gardens?'

'Yes, I did, I assure you, I…*fourteen* Dinton Gardens?'

'Yes.'

'Edwin Smith lives at 14 Dinton Gardens?'

Dominic could not believe it.

Whatever Vernon's reply was, it went unheard.

The initial knowledge that he had failed Vernon was enough – but… he had killed a perfectly innocent man. Whatever Vernon's reason for wishing Edwin Smith dead, he could accept that decision. But he had killed someone else. He could *not* live with that.

He heard Vernon again:

'Number 14 was built recently; before the plot was sold, number 12 was the last house in Dinton Gardens. They numbered the new house 14. And the owner of 12 moved into it. It was built to his specifications, Edwin Smith's specifications, and he sold number 12.'

'But his name was Edwin Smith?'

'His name was Edwin Smith and he lives at number 14.'

'But I got the wrong house?'

'Yes, you got the wrong house.'

'But I looked up E Smith's address. I found it in the telephone directory.'

'And you think that's up to date? It's out of date as soon as it's published. And was it the current edition?'

'Yes, I think so, I…' He paused. 'But Vernon, I've killed someone who…'

'Oh sorry, Dominic, I should have told you sooner; I was so wrapped up in my project. You have killed no one.'

'But I aimed…'

'With a gun loaded with blanks.'

'But why did you want me to…?'

'Dominic, what do I do for a living?'

'You're an author. And a very good one.'

'And that is because I research each book very carefully. And that is why I gave you the project to see what problems my character would encounter. To see what mistakes he would make. Edwin was happy to co-operate. But he was surprised not to see you – until that is, he noticed you patrolling the house next door.'

'He saw me?'

'Well, yes. But he was rather alarmed at your popping up at the window next door so frequently. Fortunately, he knows Philip quite well – after all he had sold his house to him.'

'So you knew all the time, and you let me…'

'Oh, yes; it was a real-life situation. It's what *could* have happened and, so, invaluable to me. I couldn't even admit what I knew after you had phoned with your news of the 'killing'. Sorry. My only worry was that blanks can sometimes injure people. But Philip kept well away from the window. And I suspected you wouldn't aim straight anyway.'

'So, you let me believe all that?'

'Yes, yes, but Dominic, when *The Riddle of Dack Street* is published, you will know that you made a major contribution to it.'

'But I didn't. I failed. I made mistakes. I killed the wrong person.'

'Yes, you are human. And that's what humans do. And you have done me a great service. You have made a major contribution to the story. The murderer now murders the wrong man. I hadn't thought of that story line.'

'So, I was invaluable?'

'Absolutely.'

That praise gave him some pleasure without restoring, completely, his faith in his friend. This had been fast disappearing.

And Dominic was unsure that he would trust Vernon so implicitly in future. In fact, he was not sure that he would see so much of him.

He put down the phone and settled in his chair.

He reached for a book – his sole solace in times of trouble. Dominic Beecher was unsure that he was cut out to be a criminal and any involvement in criminal activity would, in future, be his reading of detective novels. However, he knew that there was one

book he would never purchase, would never read:
The Riddle of Dack Street.

The New Eight Bells

Her clothes were soaked through. It was only light rain, but it had rained steadily all day. And she had been *out* all day – looking. Looking but not finding.

'Do you need help?'

Geraldine did not need any help. She shook her head and walked on as if no one had spoken.

'I could help.'

She was irritated. How did he know he could help when he didn't know what, or whom, she was seeking? Or indeed whether she was searching at all.

'I saw her at the New Eight Bells.'

She looked up for the first time.

'She was waiting for someone. It might have been you. I can show you.'

'I know where the New Eight Bells is.'

It may have been an attempt to be helpful, but she did not intend to show any gratitude. Particularly since he clearly *did* know what she was doing – and, possibly, for whom she was looking.

She walked on and he made to follow.

'I could show you.'

'I have told you that I know where the New Eight Bells is. I do not need your help.'

He watched as she walked away.

The sky was blackening, and she looked up. The dark clouds

threatened heavier rain.

She walked faster – towards the New Eight Bells.

He could follow; she feared he would follow. As the rain came down harder, her dress became more saturated. She was not dressed for this type of rain. She risked a look behind. He had not followed her, but he still stood, watching her.

She entered the bar at the New Eight Bells. It was one of few country inns which had not been subject to a modern make-over – to make it look older. It did not need to look older than its five hundred years.

She looked around.

She could see no one that she knew. An elderly couple nursed wine glasses in their hands and men took a few moments from drinking their beer to look at the newcomer. Her dress was plastered to her body, making her annoyed at their stares. She returned them, however, challenging them to smile or make a comment. None did.

Cecilia was not there. Had he lied? Or had she simply left?

She shrugged and opened the door. He was standing there in the rain, turning her annoyance to anger. But still she did not speak. She brushed by him on the narrow path. Why had he followed her? She wanted to know why he had directed her as he had, whether he had really seen the girl for whom she was looking.

But she would not ask. And, this time, he did not follow her.

'She *was* there; she must have left,' he called to her retreating back.

Since he had not entered the inn, she wondered how he could know the girl was no longer there.

Which told her something – that he had mis-directed her, but not why he had done so – or how he had known of her quest.

There again – oh, she wrenched a small branch off a tree and hurled it ahead of her.

He was still there. Staring after her.

103

Geraldine removed her wet clothes. As she showered, she thought of the man who had intercepted her on her walk. It was clearly no coincidental meeting; he had expected her and had had information ready for her about a friend with whom he must have been somehow acquainted.

But, somehow, as the weeks progressed, she was losing her fear of him. Was it his helpfulness? After all she left the inn after a quick look round; it must have been obvious that she had not found Cecilia there. And he had not followed her back.

She wondered whether she could trust him, his kindly looks having begun to make the impression he presumably hoped they would. And she had greater worries than a man who had shown no aggression towards her and represented, she felt, little threat. She had Cecilia to worry about. Cecilia and she had attended the same school and had become close. They attended the same clubs and met frequently. Because Cecilia, like Geraldine, was not easily frightened, Geraldine took very seriously her phone calls and her occasional visits, during which her friend claimed that she was being followed, and that her privacy was being invaded.

Geraldine rang Cecilia's number. The reply startled her; there was panic in her voice.

'He's in the garden.'

'Celia, try to speak calmly; what can I do? I will come over now.'

There was no reply.

'Celia?'

'Yes, yes; I'm... Yes, please come over. The police haven't come yet – I've phoned them.'

Geraldine put on her raincoat and braved the last of the rain. It was quicker to walk than to take the circuitous route by car. As she left the house, she saw the man who had met her near the New Eight Bells. He did not appear to be waiting for her, just returning from the inn.

As she passed him, he said:

'Sorry, I seem... I'm not... Anyway I'm sorry; I only meant

to help.'

Perhaps he did – and he did not follow her. Neither did he stop to watch her as on the previous occasion, but walked on past, more quickly than he had previously done.

Geraldine did not speak to him and rushed by without looking at him. Even if he were enamoured of her, and Geraldine had been given many indications that her beauty was noticed by men, his importance in her life was less than the situation in which Cecilia found herself.

And she walked quickly, barely noticing the rain which had become a light misty drizzle.

Cecilia's house was at the end of an unmade driveway, but she ignored the mud with which her legs were becoming spattered.

She rang the bell but, clearly, Cecilia had been waiting by the door, so quickly did she answer it.

Geraldine had never seen Cecilia like this. She clasped her friend who put her arms around her. Cecilia ignored the dampness of Geraldine's coat, embraced her more tightly and cried onto her shoulder.

Geraldine had never seen her cry, had never seen her shake with fear.

'Where is he?' she asked.

'Somewhere in the garden,' Cecilia said.

'I'll see. The police?'

'They've not come yet.'

Cecilia seemed reluctant to release her friend from their embrace. But she did, and Geraldine crept slowly to the back of the house.

'He is wearing a blue and white coat. He always does,' Cecilia said irrelevantly. Geraldine moved further towards the conservatory, ignoring this information. If there was a man in it, the colours of his coat were not germane to her quest.

Her heart beating loudly, and with Cecilia hanging on to her coat, Geraldine carefully pushed the door that led into the conservatory. She moved forward. There was nowhere in it to hide. She passed through it and into the garden.

'There's no one here now,' she said, carefully searching the garden.

Cecilia pulled her back, through the conservatory and into the lounge where Geraldine removed her coat.

'We must wait for the police,' she said.

The ring at the bell indicated that the wait was over.

She had rung more than once before, when she had felt threatened, and been told that, if the man in blue and white – as she had begun to call him – came again, she must call them. Although their approach was kindly, the message this time was the same. There was not much they could do, they told her, until they were in a position to apprehend him.

On their departure, Cecilia said: 'They don't believe me, anyway.'

'You don't know that.'

Cecilia sighed:

'They act as if they don't, and they treat me like an anxious female.'

There was little Geraldine could say although the fear her friend had shown when Geraldine had arrived was not that of an 'anxious female' but of someone suffering abject fear, a normally well-adjusted woman driven to her extremity.

'Well, they can put a guard on the house.'

'They can't; they don't have enough manpower apparently.'

'So, they will wait until you are attacked and then come to find your body?'

Geraldine realised that this sentiment could have been expressed more delicately.

'Well, I will stay with you tonight.'

'But,' said Cecilia, 'you have your own life. You have your own problems.'

A week passed without a visit from the man in blue and white. Geraldine was less troubled, too, by the man she had met on her walk to the New Eight Bells. Indeed, living in the area, their paths had crossed on more than one occasion without Geraldine feeling threatened by him.

As the weather improved, and Geraldine took to walking more often in the country, she saw him more often. He clearly enjoyed country walks as much as she did.

And, as their meetings increased, on one of them, he did speak:

'Forgive me, I should not invade your privacy but may I ask: Is your friend OK?'

Surprised, Geraldine queried how he knew about her friend.

'We are a chummy lot in the New Eight Bells; it is difficult not to know people. If you went in there more often, you'd be a part of it. Although I know Cecilia only by sight – and Clive by reputation.'

'Clive?'

'Yes. He is a monster; he… I think Cecilia knows him as the man in blue and white.'

'But "Clive" and Cecilia frequent the same pub?'

'I've never seen Clive in there. But I hear about him by listening to conversations. Not people I associate with, but I hear them talking – a little group that seem to regard women as "fair game". "If they dress like that…" You know the sort of thing? My friends hate them, but that does not stop them picking up what they say and reporting it.'

Geraldine nodded.

'I could help,' the man said.

Geraldine smiled, and nodded again but walked on, paused and said over her shoulder:

'How can you help?'

'A man around is better defence against a, well, let's give him the benefit of the doubt, and call him a stalker.'

Geraldine ignored his offer although his charm was having an effect on her. How was it that a man she so distrusted on their early meetings was becoming someone she felt she might be able to trust? She was beginning to attribute her early feelings towards him as a general fear of men in the light of the man who was disturbing Cecilia's life. This man, 'her' man as she was beginning to call him, was proving to be very different. Perhaps he *could* help. Perhaps she could trust him.

But it was some time before the man had gained Geraldine's confidence sufficiently for his invitation to have a drink in the New Eight Bells to be accepted. And it was then that she had learnt how he had left the inn shortly after seeing Cecilia on the occasion of his first meeting with Geraldine.

'Your friend – I've seen you together – was there when I left.'

'But how did you know I was looking for her?'

'She had asked for you at the bar. She had asked for Geraldine. When I saw you clearly looking for someone, it seemed obvious who you were – and whom you were looking for.'

His kindness and obvious fondness for her was eroding her feeling of fear and apprehension that she had felt on their early meetings.

And lunches at the New Eight Bells became a regular occurrence. So regular that Geraldine invited the man to her house.

Together they planned what they were going to do about 'Clive', the man in blue and white. While 'Clive' had not yet worried Cecilia again, he was to do so one October evening:

'He is there?' the man had asked. Geraldine relayed her friend's side of the telephone conversation.

'He is in the garden. I know he is there,' Cecilia said.

'Keep her talking,' he said. 'While she is talking on the phone, Clive won't leave. He knows you are not coming over while you are still on the phone. I will get round there. Has she phoned the police?'

Geraldine nodded and her companion left.

'Is he still there?' she asked her friend.

'Yes, of course he's still here. Do you think I…?' she said angrily.

'Celia, I think you have to be sure he is…'

'He's here. He's…' The pitch of her voice increased. She suddenly stopped.

'Celia! Celia.'

'He's coming at me. He's…'

She screamed.

After 'Clive's' latest appearance, Cecilia and Geraldine sat round a table at the New Eight Bells. Geraldine had her arm round her friend's shoulder while Freeman (she had learned that this was his Christian and not his surname) brought drinks.

He had said that he would leave them while Geraldine comforted her friend. And he made no attempt to make his usual efforts to manoeuvre to the bar ahead of those also seeking drinks.

'What happened? I only heard it on the phone.'

'I'm so sorry, I thought you had begun to doubt me.'

'Never mind about that,' said Geraldine, 'you were upset.'

'But I shouted at you. I raged at you.'

'I think I might well have done the same had the man in blue and white been coming at me.'

'Well,' Cecilia said, returning to her friend's question, 'he had been hiding for a while; then he would appear before me – then disappear again. I was just… I'm so sorry, I…'

'Shhh. And then what happened?'

'There was a sound at the window. I knew the man wasn't there. So I thought there were two of them. Then the second man…'

'Freeman.'

'Freeman. Then Freeman appeared. And he ran towards where I had last seen the man in blue and white.'

'Clive.'

'Yes, I can't call him that, but…'

'What happened, Celia? What happened next?'

'I heard a lot of noise – a fight, well that's what it sounded like. The man who'd come in the window – Freeman – came into the room. I was just as frightened.'

'But he calmed you. He told me he had calmed you. But he didn't tell me about the fight. That's the sort of man he is.'

Freeman returned to the table with drinks.

'Suffice to say you won't see Clive again,' he said to Cecilia.

Geraldine placed her hand on his.

Geraldine lay comfortably back.

'You are the most beautiful girl I…'

'Yes, you can stay the night!'

'Well, I shouldn't have asked.'

'You didn't have to.'

Geraldine smiled and climbed the stairs.

There was something in Freeman's attitude which had changed. He was no longer the man with whom she had calmly talked over the previous weeks. The charm was gone. The caring attitude: all gone.

'You are hurting me.'

'I like hurting you,' he said.

She struggled:

'No, I don't want this.'

'You are going to have this.'

Geraldine screamed, but the cottage was detached. There was no one to hear. She tried to escape him but there was no escape. She realised she was in greater danger than Cecilia had been.

Geraldine's struggles continued, but he easily conquered her.

She lay on the floor. Her face was cut; her body was bruised, and her mind was assailed by fear.

He stood above her.

She lay with her hands over her face. He came at her again. She felt his fists…

After dragging her downstairs, he flung her onto the floor.

110

He sat comfortably over her as if embarking upon a friendly conversation.

'Well, there are one or two things I need to sort out.'

'If you left me, I'd not...'

'Oh, no I won't be leaving. I've enjoyed this evening too much. Firstly, I should tell you that my name's not Freeman. Who would believe that anyone had a forename of Freeman? Everyone, or all those who matter, have always known me as Freeman, but...'

He laughed and continued.

'But that doesn't matter to you. What matters to you is that you will have a house mate for some considerable time. You have kindly told me that you are an orphan. That's good; no family to worry about you – and foster parents who have long left the scene. You see that I have found out all the things I need to know about you – including that uncle who never saw you when you needed him but left you everything he had when he died. So, you have no job. Lazy that. Living on ill-gotten gains. But that makes things easy. Now we have one problem: Cecilia. Your friend. Your very close friend. But, really, that problem is easily solved.

'Clive will help me there.'

Geraldine gasped.

'Oh, yes, you really didn't think I had a fight with my best mate, did you? Clive will sort Cecilia out. I don't know what he'll do. Wouldn't it be funny if he's doing exactly the same with your friend as I am going to do with you?'

Geraldine looked up in even greater alarm.

'Oh yes; I'm going to keep you in storage – take you out when I need a little enjoyment and store you away ready for next time. Oh, don't worry; you'll be well fed. And will anyone believe you when I've finished with you? That's if anyone ever sees you. I may just keep you. No need to ever let you go really is there? And much safer.

'And where am I going to keep you?' he asked. 'No, that's a rhetorical question – I'll tell you. You were so kind as to show me the whole house. You were quite keen to show me how you had spent the money your dear – well not so dear – uncle left you. And that basement – so convenient. And I've bought some lovely bolts for the door. And every time I pass those steps I can think of you – so sweetly waiting for me. Any time I like.'

He laughed.

'Now, would you like to walk quietly down there – or will I have to drag you down, kicking and screaming? Now that would be fun, wouldn't it?'

Geraldine rose carefully from the floor and, cowed, walked away from him and to the door of the cellar. She opened the door and entered. Once he had closed it, she could hear him fixing the lock and bolting the door.

And then she sat.

And cried.

Like she had never cried before.

But she cried tears of relief, not of despair.

She sat for over an hour until she became calmer. She could not, of course, relax with a monster upstairs. But she could think. She knew what would be in store for her; the experience she had already suffered had been terrifying. And she felt it would be as nothing to what he was planning.

But she was less worried. How convenient that he had chosen for her prison a basement with an exit.

Not an exit about which he could possibly know the existence. She gently lifted the boxes in the corner and felt the handle of the door which, she knew, issued onto a narrow passage. That passage was skirted on both sides by a high flint wall.

She heard him moving outside the cellar door and quickly moved the boxes back. She had no doubt that his enjoyment involved reminding her that he was there. All the time. She heard him jiggle the lock and slide the bolt. She crept to the door and listened, hearing his steps up the stairs from the cellar. She could even hear him laughing.

Slowly, and keeping her attention on the cellar door, she unstacked the boxes again and opened the door to the passage. The key turned slowly – and she feared the door might not open. But it did, despite having been unused for many years. Her greatest fear now was the creaking noise its hinges emitted. She looked over her shoulder at the cellar door, worried that he might enter the cellar.

But she heard nothing from him. From the passage, she stacked the boxes back and pushed the door to, locking it from the outside and slipping the key into the pocket of her dress.

She walked slowly along the passage, constantly looking over her shoulder. No one appeared at the passage door and all she needed to do was to exit the passage and make for open country. She knew he would try to find her; he had too much to lose by her freedom. But she should be able to make her way to Cecilia's house. Although he had deprived her of her mobile phone, she could ring the police from there – providing Cecilia was alone.

She turned the corner and stared to the end of the passage.

At a man in a blue and white coat.

And To The Wicker Bridge

She sat on the seat and remembered. Old Art would have been her present age. She smiled as she recalled hearing of a love affair that had happened such a long time ago. She relaxed in her seat and the soporific effect of the sun and the air caused her to sleep and recall the day when, as a young girl, she had met the old man:

Old Art sat under the afternoon sun and lit his pipe, settling into the seat he had occupied every afternoon since retiring twenty years before. Now he pulled out his watch and shook his head sadly. Annette was seldom late.

Art hardly noticed the click of high heels along the park avenue - there were so many passers-by - but on this occasion the clicking stopped and a girl sat on the seat beside him. Art turned, disinterestedly at first, but his first glance caused him to look more carefully. For the girl could have been Annette as she had been sixty six years before - just out of school and beautiful as the afternoon.

There were differences of course. This girl dressed very differently to Annette; the skirt which had ridden up around her thighs revealed long sun-tanned legs, secrets which Annette had kept hidden from him. But the face. The face took him back and he felt like a boy again.

'Have you been waiting long?' she said.

'You speak like her too,' Art mumbled.

'I beg your pardon?'

'Like Annette, you speak like Annette.' Art felt foolish, remembering the girl was a stranger.

'I'm sorry: you will not know of course.'

'Annette? I think so. Was that Grandmother's name?'

'Your grandmother? Of course. You are so like her.'

'From what I have heard, that is a compliment.'

'Yes, she was beautiful, quite beautiful, I... Why has she sent you? Is she ill?'

'Well no,' the girl said staring out into the park.

Art smiled at her. Well if she was not ill...

'Why did you come? Where is she?'

'I don't know how to tell you.'

'No, don't,' he said quickly. 'Don't tell me. I know.' The girl did not know what to say. She looked at the ground and then at Art.

'I'm sorry.' she said.

'Yes, yes, thank you. I'm sorry. You look so like her that, but for your clothes...'

The girl smiled and waited for the old man to speak.

'That's where Annette was,' Art said suddenly, pointing.

'I beg your pardon?'

'Annette - when I met her. She was over by the fountain.'

The girl smiled again:

'Nothing can have changed since then - in the park I mean.'

'No,' he said. 'I think that's why we always met here. Nothing changed. Still nothing changes.'

'When did you meet? Would you tell me?'

He smiled: 'The exact day? Some people would remember that. But somehow I can't. Then, you see, it was a terrible sin.' He looked down as if in shame.

'She was married,' he continued.

'Yes she was.'

'And to a pillar of society.'

'Grandfather?' she laughed. 'Was he?'

'Oh yes. But you never met him?'

'No, of course. But I heard about him and he did not sound like a pillar of society.'

'Who told you about him? Annette?'

'No, she never talked about him. My other grandfather knew him. He thought he was a...'

'Yes, some people did not like him and, of course, I never could.'

'But why did you never marry? He died so young.'

'Yes he did. And she never loved him. But somehow... We met every afternoon you see. She worked in the shop and I was always free. But somehow the guilt remained. Even after he was dead. Our meetings were always somehow clandestine. I don't know how to explain it.'

She smoothed her hand down her legs and drew them up towards her, noticing the old man's obvious but unspoken admiration. She smiled:

'You were wondering whether your Annette had legs like these?'

Art laughed.

'You seem to know my thoughts. It must come from being related - to Annette I mean.' He sighed.

'You are much more sensible. You young. Some say your behaviour is unacceptable, but you don't suffer as we suffered.' He looked at the legs which she had again stretched out before her.

'I'm sorry if I upset you,' the girl said.

'No, no. But that was precisely why we...'

'Met as you did?'

'Yes. I went away to the city. But I saw her a lot. Then he died. And it was somehow... harder. He was more of an obstacle dead than alive.' He put his pipe into his pocket. Again he was silent and she prompted him.

'Oh, we met now and then; it seemed like no time later I was sixty five and they retired me. Then I came back here. And we began to meet again just as we had before.'

'But you still never married?'

'No, I don't think it occurred to us. We came here and we held…'

'You held hands?'

'Yes. Does that sound silly?'

'No, it sounds lovely. It must be lovely to be in love at sixty five.'

'Oh and at seventy, and at eighty. Always in love.'

She smiled.

'And what else did you do?'

'Oh sometimes we walked. Down to the wicker bridge.'

'The wicker bridge?'

'Yes. It's not there now. It's one of the few things that have changed. I think we still felt we were doing wrong but we didn't care. Not then.'

The girl laughed and took his hand.

'You must have been happy then.'

'Yes, I think we were. I think for the first time we were really happy.'

Again he was silent. Then she noticed that his eyes were closed. He was smiling and she heard his breathing becoming fainter. The park was silent except for the rustling of the faint breeze in the trees. She looked up at the cloudless sky and the heat haze by the fountain where the old people had met. She wondered about her grandmother and her lover, about their meetings and their guilt. Then he felt her gentle hand before he clasped both hands together in his lap. She thought he had said 'Annette' before his head slumped against the wrought iron head rest of the seat. But she could have been mistaken.

Dorothea

Ephraim walked on, around the puddles and mud patches. The fluffy clouds of the morning had darkened and the sky had become an uninterrupted dark grey. But there was very little point in going back home; there would be no one there.

He watched a man pushing a bicycle up the steep hill. Ephraim was surprised to see that, on the cyclist's noticing him, he mounted his bicycle and struggled to climb the hill. Ephraim had caught only a passing glimpse of the man, as he looked sharply round, but he noticed a look of fear on the cyclist's face. Why should the man fear him? Ephraim had not lived in the area long and did not socialise; even so he felt that he had seen the man about. And the cyclist's anxiety and hurry to depart, despite the steepness of the road, showed that he had no desire to be recognised, something which caused Ephraim no disappointment since he did not wish him to stay. However, while Ephraim did not want this man's company, the current uncertainty surrounding his own life made him worry about the cyclist's actions.

Ephraim thought the darkening sky presaged worsening weather.

As if to confirm this forecast, large drops of rain began to fall. Perhaps he *should* go home. But then Dorothea was no longer there. It would make him think of her and he didn't wish to.

Ephraim walked back down the lane, the rain beginning to run down his neck as it came down harder. He looked round once and the cyclist was vanishing round the bend at the top of the hill.

Before Ephraim turned off the road, he looked back - but the man had gone. Ephraim was sure that the cyclist's presence on the road at the same moment as himself had been no coincidence – the man's nervousness and desire to escape attention was obvious. He increased his pace and turned left down another lane, partly to double back to his house, partly to deter pursuit. It was a straight lane and he would have seen the man behind him, particularly if he were riding. But he was reassured that he had not been followed and struck on at a fast walk.

As Ephraim put on the kettle, the rain was slapping hard against the window and the wind – negligible before – whooped intermittently. It was going to be a wild night. He looked with sorrow and fear at the newly made mound of earth in the garden. He missed Dorothea; how he now wished to speak to her.

The incident with the cyclist still worried him. What if the cyclist had kept out of sight and followed him? He took his tea into the front conservatory and looked out. If the man had followed him, he was not to be seen now. Ephraim, guessing at his occupancy of a neighbouring house, assumed that the cyclist knew where he lived anyway. He sat with his tea, looking out aimlessly at the rain swirling against the glass of the conservatory.

Ephraim woke to a misty country morning. The rain would not hold off long; the sky was turning lamp black. Soon the rain came - heavy rain; there had been rain for several days. He looked into the back garden, at the rectangle of disturbed earth, with the raised mound above it.

And then he saw what he had dreaded. The man he had seen in the lanes. By the time Ephraim had approached the back door, the man had seen him and vanished. He was taking an unhealthy interest in Ephraim's affairs.

Was it wise to leave the house unoccupied, since the cyclist had entered his garden to appear beside a specific area of it? Wise or not, Ephraim was unable to tie himself to the house and he could certainly not move anything from the garden given the apparent observation he was under. He spent the rest of the day at the back of the house, inspecting the garden to see if the man returned. He did not.

Could he lie in wait for the cyclist's next visit and accost him? If he could do that, was there anything that Ephraim could do to deter further visits? He was reluctant to take a violent approach, but it was his only course. Otherwise he would have to continue – as he had done for some days – to sleep downstairs and endure a state of siege. And he lived in fear. He had run to the front door when he had heard a sound, to quickly return to his observation of the back. He regretted not increasing the security of the cottage when he had moved into it a short while ago. Whether it was the situation preying on his mind or not, he had become convinced that there had, several times, been someone in the house.

The November weather was sufficiently inclement for him to go on only rare sentry duties outside the house. Whether the man would be deterred by the wind and rain he doubted, but spending days in the open could not help *his* spirits.

And the unsettling number of unfamiliar noises, both inside and outside the house, increased. He tried to convince himself that, living in an old country cottage, such noises were not unusual. But he had not heard them before. He had not heard footsteps seemingly descending the stairs, or dull thuds emanating from the loft. He had not heard the sound of a key being inserted in the front door.

Ephraim was convinced that each noise was made to unsettle him, not necessarily to gain access to – or to search - the house, but he was sure that someone *was* inside the house.

One day, Ephraim saw again the figure in the garden and crept carefully towards him. It was the man he had seen in the lanes. Ephraim's eyes moved between him and the rectangle of disturbed earth by which he stood.

Without any particular plan in mind – despite the number of times he had thought what he should do in this situation – Ephraim approached the man before he could escape. He grasped his collar and threw him to the ground.

'What are you doing here?' Ephraim angrily shouted into his face.

The man was obviously searching for some reason which would satisfy his assailant.

'Er... is Dorothea in?' he said, immediately regretting his stupidity in doing so.

'Dorothea is not in because she has left me. She has gone to France,' Ephraim told the man.

'Well, it is sad that I cannot see her. It would have been nice. She always had a friendly word for me,' he lied. 'But I don't need to see her. I will go now; please let me go.'

Ephraim's anger overcame him. He put both hands round the man's neck and shook his head in his fury, but the man pushed back, kicking out. For some moments they struggled; then Ephraim – getting the upper hand – hit him fiercely. He looked at the body lying prone on the ground. He could see, with relief, that the man was breathing and dragged him into the house and down into the cellar, where he pulled a chair into its only room and began to tie a rope around him.

He taped the man's mouth and hands with duct tape. He searched him for weapons, finding none; he removed a mobile phone from the man's pocket but was unable to unlock it. However, keeping it avoided the probability that the man would use it to obtain assistance. He further searched for items which would identify the man but, again, he drew a blank. He waited for him to recover consciousness. After some time he did so.

'You will stay here,' he said, convinced that the man's bonds allowed no other possibility. The look of fear on the cyclist's face reminded him of the horror he had displayed when Ephraim had seen him pushing his bike.

And Ephraim did now feel safe in leaving the cottage –

and he did so, driving to a supermarket where he bought the provisions which he had lacked since his self-imposed confinement. He bought extra for the man: he had no wish for him to die of hunger.

On his return, he went to the cellar to find the man as he had left him. He removed the tape from his mouth and was pleased to see that there was no diminution in the look of terror on the man's face. He did not speak, just stared. Ephraim could think of nothing to say, so he prepared food for them both, and fed the man in the cellar. The prisoner ate mechanically before Ephraim restored the gag. Ephraim loosened the ropes around his legs and took him to the toilet on the floor above. He saw no reason to provide any further exercise for the man, re-tying the ropes more tightly than before.

The dark weather continued; the wind howled like a pack of wolves and the rain continued to saturate an already waterlogged garden. He looked at the disturbed area of earth and thought the rain would make digging easier but he made no attempt to take advantage of the opportunity it offered for moving the contents of the hole.

He thought that perhaps he could come and go without hindrance now but was careful not to leave the cottage for too long, not being confident the man in the cellar was his only enemy. When one day he returned, he realised his worst fears had been justified. The front door was open. He did not hesitate, did not look to see how a door he had locked on departing now swung on its hinges. His immediate concern was the basement, to which he ran. He flung open the door of the room in which he had left the man. He was still there.

Ephraim ripped the tape from his face:

'What has happened?'

The man stared. His face again showed fear but, now, also bafflement. Ephraim replaced the tape and went to close the front door.

It was only the first intrusion. And it confirmed that the man in the basement was not the only one to be interested in his activities. Ephraim took to sleeping downstairs again and the noises of the house continued to assail him. Doors within the cottage, which he had closed, were opened. His property was moved, his movement monitored. His office was ransacked during the night and then, one night, he heard the cellar door open. He slowly crept toward the stairs from which the footsteps emanated. And, from the darkness, a figure emerged. He flattened himself into an alcove and watched the figure pass by him. It was a man and he recognised that man; it was someone who had shared long hours of planning with him, who had worked towards the same objective. It was a man who had trusted him but whom he had betrayed. He listened intently and heard the front door close. He then went down into the cellar. Still secured in the chair was the man he had brought in from the garden. It was as if the intruder were escaping from *him*.

He expected a return of the intruder since he had obviously not found what he sought – and, in early light, he heard the turning of the front door handle. He sank behind a settee and watched. The door opened slowly and a figure walked into the cottage.

It was not a man. It was a woman.

'Dorothea,' he shouted.

Dorothea, for it was indeed she, walked towards him.

'I thought I told you not to come back here,' Ephraim said.

Dorothea nodded. She held out to him a newspaper in which, on the front page, was the story of a major theft. Of enough silver and gold to make a man – or woman, or both – immensely rich.

She embraced him:

'I carried out our plan, arranging the route we would take, finding a fence, arranging a price, but...'

'But...'

'But someone found me. I don't know how – I must have been followed.'

Ephraim knew it could only have been his partner in the burglary, the man he had since seen on the stairs from the cellar. He knew now how foolish he had been not to just split the haul.

Indeed he would have given anything to turn back the clock and never to have committed the burglary at all:

'What did he do?' he said.

'He offered to share the proceeds with me if I would reveal where the haul was. And he wanted to go away with me.'

Ephraim sat down and motioned for Dorothea to do the same, saying:

'He didn't know where the… where it all was?'

'I don't think so. He wouldn't have needed to ask me – or to pretend to want my company - if so. Can we still move it? I could find another buyer – not so easy now, but we could…'

Ephraim held her hand: 'No, that's not possible. For I think that man will soon know where it is. He certainly knows where I live now. And there is another reason.'

Dorothea was silent. She followed him as he led her to the cellar and to the man Ephraim had brought in from the garden.

Ephraim had never seen a man so startled.

'Dorothea!' he said.

Dorothea peered at the man, surprised - not only that the man knew her name but that he was imprisoned in a chair in their basement. She was trying to identify him, could not, and asked:

'Do you know me?'

'No, but I have seen pictures of you. We checked.'

'Who checked?'

The man, as far as he could, held out his hands for release. Ephraim shrugged and started to untie the man's bonds.

'We, ah, the police had a report - a tip off.'

Ephraim and Dorothea waited.

'Ephraim was seen in the garden, burying a large box – well, the informant told us it was "like a coffin".'

Hope surged in Ephraim and Dorothea's breasts. They were careful to say nothing.

It was an impossible story to believe. No police officer would linger at a crime scene while in danger of being observed by the criminal. He would have reported and brought a party to search the garden. Neither would his colleagues have failed to look for him when he did not return. The real story was that he was a sufficiently near neighbour to observe Dorothea over a long period – with strong binoculars. Dorothea was a beautiful woman and it was his greatest pleasure to watch her going about her daily routines. Somehow, he felt, she was available – within reach. He would dream about her. And it was he who had witnessed Ephraim's 'burial' in the garden which, without the aid of binoculars, no one would have seen. Everything he had done since then had been to confirm his belief that Ephraim had murdered and buried his wife. Having proved that this crime had taken place, he would have reported his 'neighbour' to the police.

The ludicrousness of the claim that this man was a policeman encouraged Ephraim to ask him: 'Since you have now seen Dorothea, do you intend to leave us in peace? You can now leave; we will do nothing. You can understand my anger and my having to, ah, incarcerate you.'

'Yes, indeed, I was wrong; you were perfectly justified.' The man was beginning to recover his confidence: 'Er, while I apologise for the intrusion, you will be able to understand it – and, after all, you need only have dug up that patch and shown me that Dorothea was not at the bottom of the hole.'

'I suppose so,' Ephraim said doubtfully, 'so, if we release you – which we are going to do – your interest in the affair is over?'

'Oh, of course; the police (Ephraim was surprised that he continued to claim that he was a police officer) have no interest in your gardening. And *I* don't need to know.'

He gave Ephraim a worried look because he had noticed Ephraim's hesitation in his task of untying the ropes. Ephraim looked at Dorothea. Dorothea shook her head:

'No, I don't think there is any point leaving him bound; as you said, we can't carry on with this. There is someone else who will soon know what we have in the garden. And the police *will* be told and won't leave us alone, even if we remove everything and move away. And our accomplice is making sure that continuing to live in this cottage is impossible.'

Ephraim had not really needed Dorothea to tell him that. He knew his hesitation was prompted by a desperate hope that all their planning should not come to nothing. And he knew what the alternative was – the inevitable consequence of failure. He simply said:

'Someone saw me burying something. It was damned bad luck.'

Dorothea sighed: 'Damned bad luck.'

The Record Shop

Somehow – in retrospect – the sun was always shining in the London superb in which I grew up. I imagine it did rain, but I can't remember that. The garden is always golden in my memory, the bees are buzzing round the clover in the lawn, making its last appearance before my father mowed it, and trimmed the privet hedge to a perfect shape.

The way to the high street led past the impressive Art Deco cinema and, crossing the road, to what was colloquially – but not officially - known as the Bus Stop Fields. Here German bombs had left a derelict area which nature had already claimed, and small hills and valleys had made it a natural playground for us.

The name was derived from the bus terminus which lay alongside, from which I would make weekly journeys on the 691 trolley bus to my grandparents' house.

Continuing up the high street one came to a large – or so it seemed to my young eyes - record shop with a huge collection of records arranged on shelves behind the counter which ran the length of the shop. I have not seen since quite so many records in one place.

The Record Shop, as it was named, was a meeting place for those who attended my school and the bare boarded floor area was such that, at weekends, it would host small concerts with youngsters dancing to the music of the record player.

We would congregate there after school to listen to the

music Old Joe (in retrospect he was probably not very old at all) would 'spin'. By about five o'clock, the music – mostly requested by the schoolboys – would be continuous.

'Is the new Eddie Cochran in?'

'Has there been a new Buddy Holly?' Since Buddy Holly had been dead for over a year, these 'new' records were mostly issued from old tapes which were continually being found, an added soundtrack justifying the name 'new'.

'Play Say Mama – Gene Vincent – please Joe.'

There was a special section for ex-juke box records – very popular because very cheap. Providing one was willing to buy 'middles' to replace those which were removed for their use in the juke box. This did not stop many of us gathering around the long wooden boxes in which the juke box records were stored - for they were in good condition, not having suffered the mis-use which was evident on the scratchy discs available in the second hand store up the road.

Each day, after release from school at 3.50., I would join the gathering to hear – and request – the latest songs. If some girls entered the shop, some would dance but we mostly listened, and scanned the endless seeming rows of discs in cardboard sleeves which would be replaced by the appropriate coloured paper cover when a purchase was made.

But there was one other reason we would gather there in such numbers:

Sonia.

Sonia was Old Joe's daughter and worked at The Record Shop. She seemed a lot older than us but was probably only about eighteen. Sonia can be seen through the years – and I am sure my recollections of her are shared with many of my school fellows. But I have always felt that I had greater reason to remember her than my friends could ever boast.

Sonia never went out of her way to appeal to those who adored her. She was just... Sonia. Sonia would sell records but also would walk round the shop when sales were slow, advising and finding requested songs. At these times she would hand a display copy to the prospective purchaser with the advice to 'pay at the counter please'.

With the strange trick that memory plays, it is the most inconsequential moments that one recalls. Such as the *Bolero* record cover that featured the torso of a belly dancer in a costume which did not conceal her charms. Sonia took the record and moved it to the back of the display saying that it made her feel cold. The smile on her face on returning to that display box, when the record had been restored to its prominent place at the front, indicated that she had done it for the fun it would cause. And did she, I wonder, realise that everyone in the shop was imagining Sonia so dressed?

It was one Saturday morning that I got to know Sonia better. In my hand, as I walked towards The Record Shop, was a copy of a record purchased the previous evening. Seeking perfection in the components of my record collection, I detected a tinniness in its sound quality. My father, confirming this view, put it down to sibilance.

Leaving early to get to the record shop as it opened, I arrived just as Old Joe was unbolting the door. I had no wish for my 'complaint', as I viewed it, to be public knowledge.

Old Joe put the record on his turntable, which sat flush on the work area behind the counter. As I had expected, he could find no fault with it, but told me that the 'pick up on his turntable was not spring loaded'. I had no idea what this meant, but listened to his solution with some interest.

He told me to take the record to his house 'where Sonia would play it on the radiogram'. I could not quite believe what I was being invited to do, but walked the few houses along the side road from the record shop, which was situated on its corner, with the disc clutched in my hand, and an unusual spring in my step.

Nervousness came upon me as I walked up the path and increased when Joe's wife (whom I had never seen before) answered the door. I haltingly explained why I was there.

'Sonia,' she called upstairs, 'try out this record on the radiogram. Seems to be tinny.'

Sonia appeared, attired in a night dress. I handed over the record as she smiled a welcome.

'Sounds alright,' she said. 'What was wrong with it again?'

On hearing my explanation, she said that some records did sound like that.

'But get Dad to give you a replacement – or you could have your money back?'

I nodded and returned to the record shop; to me the visit to Sonia's house had been the most magical event of my life, to her it had clearly been a small matter of business. On reflection the night dress had not been revealing or anything to raise the pulse. But, following Sonia's handling of the record, I was unwilling to change it or request a refund for it.

As I opened the door, customers were already beginning to arrive. And to Old Joe's query, I said: 'She says it's alright'.

I waved the record and thanked him.

The distance in time has perhaps painted Sonia in more glowing colours than she then exhibited. I am not sure. The truth is that I now find it very difficult to summon more than a vague impression of her face.

But I can remember well the reaction of my friends to the news that I had been to Sonia's house. I am unsure how they heard about it, certainly not from me. Perhaps from Old Joe?

Even when, the following Monday, Sonia sought me out to ask me if I was happy 'about things' my companions did not ask why I had been to her house. At the time I told myself that my reason for secrecy had been my modesty; now I believe I was quite happy for there to be a mystery; perhaps the unstated suggestion of intimacy suited me? I was sure that I could detect envy.

After that Sonia unsurprisingly treated me no differently to my friends. But I revelled in the short-lived sensation that I had visited the object of their passion. Had they known in what state of dress she had greeted me, their awe would have been even greater.

I often play that record; it is in my nature to preserve my possessions in pristine condition so, despite its age and great use, I can still assess what would have been the condition of the record that caused my visit to Sonia all those years ago.

There is not a hint of tinniness, nor of sibilance.

The Tale of the Wet Clothes

The sky darkened; the rain flew in sheets across his path.

Christian looked up just as a streak of lightning lit the sky and was followed by a clap of thunder. You had to go out on days like this. If it was your job, you had to go out. Christian gave up trying to keep himself dry. No use. Too wet to bother. And Mr Lumley needed his message.

Christian rang the bell. Why wasn't the bell working? On a day like this, why was he left outside for so long? He rapped the knocker, rattled the letterbox. An elderly woman came to the door and, although shorter than Christian, appeared to look down on him from a great height.

He stepped forward but the woman put herself in his path. Quite obviously blocking his way – and extending her palm. Christian drew out the envelope; the woman held it by its edge, staring at Christian as if he were at fault for not keeping it dry.

'I'll see Mr Lumley gets this,' she said, beginning to withdraw.

'I must hand it to *him*,' he said.

'I'll see that he gets it,' she told him – emphatically.

'I have been told I must deliver it into his hands alone.'

The woman sighed and held the door open sufficiently for him to step forward, without allowing him entry, nor permitting him the luxury of stepping on the doormat, out of the rain.

'Stay there.'

He stayed there while she called to her employer.

Mr Lumley was a white haired elderly man. His welcome could not have offered a greater contrast to that of his housekeeper.

'Come in man, come in. Don't stand there in the rain,' as if it had been Christian's choice to do so.

As Christian advanced, the woman stepped back as if protecting herself from contamination – although probably simply avoiding the water which seemed to cascade from him in a shower.

'Why man,' said Mr Lumley, 'you need a drink but, before that, you need to get into some dry clothes and have a shower.'

He could scarcely have given an instruction less popular with his housekeeper.

'But,' she said.

'No, no,' said Mr Lumley, 'it's an important message; we must be very grateful to, umm…'

'Christian, sir,' said Christian.

'Christian, of course; I remember.' Mr Lumley had never heard his name before and therefore could not have forgotten it. He protested:

'No, no, not sir; please call me David.'

Christian looked round at the housekeeper and could scarcely hide a smile, while she returned his look with one of annoyance and contempt.

'The rain is easing; by the time you're ready to go, it should have dried up and you'll have a more comfortable walk home.'

When instructed to do so, the housekeeper took Christian up the stairs to the bathroom, and accepted the wet clothes he handed, having opened it very slightly, through the bathroom door. Christian could not see her but knew that her look would be one of disgust.

Sipping brandy from a cut glass goblet, Christian knew his day's work was not complete. He would be required to return a message – or a package. If the latter, he wondered – as he always did – what that package would contain.

The brandy warmed him, and Mr Lumley offered another. Christian smiled; he would not have another. He needed to get home before the next rain came and, looking out of the wide expanse of window, he could see that this would not be long.

During his walk, a package held securely under his arm in case of attempts to steal it, Christian pondered 'the job' with which he had kept himself in relative comfort for some months. Hardly riches but well above the minimum wage for which his friends laboured. More than an ordinary company messenger anyway – he knew that because he had been one. Delivering items for directors who could well deliver their own; collecting messages which could have been sent by email. This was hardly satisfying work, but the day he looked for alternative employment was the day he had been asked to collect a pizza when the normal delivery boy had had an accident on his motor bike. That was no job for a messenger.

As a result, he had answered a small ad. in the *Evening Standard* which had been placed by the Mayfair office of Harvard, Whitney & Co..

He had been invited to the premises of the company in an office block in Mayfair. Christian had worried about that: did reputable concerns have offices in Mayfair? Well, yes; of course they did, but not many operated out of one room if their wealth was honestly obtained.

No one in the office suggested he should hide the nature of his work, nor the name of his employer; indeed there was no secrecy at all – he was invited to behave as an ordinary messenger would and certainly not to hide the identities of the recipients and senders of messages. He was not to worry and he did not. But he did wonder.

Christian left his parcel with a colleague of Mr Lumley – and returned home. Then he remembered his clothes. He had not brought them from Mr Lumley's house, but then they would not have been dry. However, Christian determined upon another visit to that establishment to retrieve them at the earliest opportunity.

Indeed he did so the next day.

Christian braced himself for the welcome that Mr Lumley's housekeeper would offer him. He was relieved when Mr Lumley, himself, appeared at the door.

The clothes? Oh, yes, of course. 'Mrs Drewett; this gentleman's – ah, Christian's – clothes please. He's called for them.'

The housekeeper showed little interest, shrugged, and held her hands outwards to her side to indicate that she was unsure where they were. Mr Lumley turned to Christian:

'I am so sorry, Mr... ah, Christian, they can't be located at the moment; I'll make it my responsibility to ensure that they are cleaned, packaged up, and sent round to you. Perhaps you would let me know your address? I know the office will have it, but that will slow things down – and you know what personnel officers are like at giving out such information.'

'Are the clothes we gave you satisfactory?'

'They're, they're fine thanks.'

What bothered Christian was not the quality of the clothes he had acquired, which bore name tags of the top manufacturers, but a doubt that had been growing in his mind about the use to which his own clothes would be put. He decided to put the matter to the back of his mind and enjoy those which had replaced them. After all, he began to think he would be reluctant to part with them.

Weeks passed and his clothes did not arrive. Christian continued with his job: messages were delivered – and received - but none from or to the house of Mr Lumley. He had begun to worry – sufficiently to make another visit to Mr Lumley's house. This time, however, he did not knock on the door. He waited outside, behind a hedge, and looked out for the comings – of which there were none – and the goings, of which there were few.

But the 'goings' were interesting. The first to leave the house was a young man of about Christian's age. Despite the distance at which he viewed him and the obstruction of the hedge, behind which he hid – Christian could see that the man was similar in build and appearance to himself. A *lot* like himself.

Now, Christian was a devotee of mystery stories, and what he had learned was useful to him. If he were threatened he would be ready. And he was beginning to feel threatened.

Why had Mr Lumley kept Christian's clothes? Fiction was often based on fact and Christian knew of stories in which the criminal was able to commit a crime and ensure that another person, of similar appearance and dress, took 'the rap'.

Christian mused. What was to stop the person he so closely resembled wearing his clothes and committing a crime – a murder perhaps, a shooting? He began to believe that the man who had left Mr Lumley's house during his surveillance was about to commit an audacious crime, and that he, Christian, was to be apprehended for it.

Why had his employer gone to such lengths to ensure secrecy in distributing messages and packages when the postal services and email were perfectly adequate to achieve his ends? And why did Mr Lumley require a housekeeper whose clear purpose was to vet callers – and exclude those without proper credentials? After all, until Mr Lumley had seen him and identified him, he would not have secured admission to that house.

And what was the business of Harvard, Whitney & Co.? Where in the offices of that company was the indication of their function – what they manufactured, or what services they performed? Were they indeed a proper company? Should he check at Companies House? – although he had to admit to being unsure at present how to go about doing that check.

Christian began to be more careful about his movements. But, did he need to be? If he was to be falsely identified as a criminal, surely the more he was seen abroad the better?

One could argue that he should advertise his presence as much as he could: book in restaurants, sign visitors' books, make opportunities to speak often to friends and relatives, and even talk to complete strangers – being careful to identify himself during such conversations.

Christian's life became one of self-advertisement. Friends and relatives received more visits than previously, many more than perhaps they relished – and strangers became puzzled when Christian would name himself before embarking on conversations. And Christian was wary of callers. Could they have been sent to ensure he was 'out of the way' when required to be – when the crime was to be committed by his doppelganger?

And, almost as soon as this thought had entered his mind, Mr Lumley called. He stood on the doorstep with a package:

'I felt that I should come myself,' he said. 'Mrs Drewett was reluctant to do so and, I am not sure why, she seems to have taken a dislike to you.'

The news did not come as a surprise nor as a disappointment to Christian whose dislike of the housekeeper was perhaps even more strongly felt.

'I, on the other hand, like you lad; you resemble my son – of whom I am very fond. It was so useful, when you needed a change of clothes, because his fitted you perfectly. And I have come with good news,' Mr Lumley said: 'you have been selected to make the presentation of a valuable work of art to Mr MacQuoid, chairman, and founder, of The MacQuoid Company Ltd. He has never been able to acquire it because he has never been able to find it. There has been a lot of hole and corner business, of which you have played an important part, but we found the collector who possessed it – and bought it. Not cheap,' he laughed, 'but does Mr MacQuoid deserve cheap? No, of course not.

'I must apologise for the minor deceptions we have been obliged to play upon you. You are a smart lad and I imagine you have discovered that no such company as Harvard, Whitney & Co. exists or ever has existed. We made that up and kept everything away from head office – and all the MacQuoid company sites. The site rent on the office, your salary, and everything, cost a great deal, but it was worth it to ensure complete secrecy for the biggest event our – Mr MacQuoid's – company has ever celebrated. His seventieth birthday, the fiftieth anniversary of the company's foundation and the day MacQuoid Company Ltd. takes over its chief rival, Revelinu. And all to take place in the Albert Hall! I didn't realise *anyone* could hire the Albert Hall – not that the MacQuoid Company is *anyone*. There are to be displays showing the history of the company; the London Symphony Orchestra will be playing. Major stars will attend. It will be the event of the year and something the Albert Hall has never experienced.'

'So the box was…'

'Worth over a million! We relied on you. You repaid our trust.'

'And I am to hand it to Mr McQuoid at the Albert Hall?'

'A well-deserved honour.'

'But will I stay with the company – when the company I work for…'

'Doesn't exist! No, but you and I will be having a little talk, assessing your considerable talents, and considering which job will suit them. I can assure you that the salaries paid by the company are considerable.'

Mr Lumley then handed Christian the package of clothes.

'Don't return my son's clothes,' said Mr Lumley. He is very grateful for what you have done for the company. And I hope you will accept the job we offer you: we'd hate you to get involved in any crime rackets!' he said – bursting into loud laughter.

Facing the Future

I would walk with her, my mother. I was careful to walk on the road side of the pavement; I had been told that this protected a lady from the filth thrown up from the road. I don't remember any filth, only my mother telling me that I was growing up to be a man. I wasn't; I could only have been eleven, just having started secondary school, where I knew no one. The protection was entirely on my mother's side. But I walked proudly; I believed I was protecting the person I revered most.

Perhaps it was only in later years, when I looked at her picture, that I realised just how beautiful she was. Even if I had been aware of that then it could not have affected my feelings for her. She was my mother; I was as proud of her as she was of me.

She was my haven from a largely friendless school. It was only later that I made new friends, took them home and proudly introduced them to her.

Growing up, she gave me the strength I needed to approach interviews; her boy was applying for a job. She communicated her pride and dried my tears when I failed. There were other jobs; I was just not suited to that one. If I persevered, I should get the job that suited me. And I did. From humble beginnings I did.

When my mother grew older and suffered from ill-health she weathered it and I believe it was my brother and I who gave her the strength to carry on. She lived for us and through us.

I have these thoughts when I sit in my chair – my window seat – looking over the garden which is maintained by a man who comes in weekly to mow the lawn and keep the flower beds trim. I see not only my current garden but the one of my youth, the trellis between the lean-to and the lawn, worn thin in places where my brother and I stood to play tennis. Where my mother would bring out drinks which we would drink in the sunshine. I do remember the glorious sunny days, but my memories are not selective; I remember the smog of London – the days my mother would wrap a scarf around our faces so that we did not breathe in the soot and smoke as we walked to school.

I still have her picture on the wall. I still have her memory etched in my mind. Without a faith, without any belief, I can gain no comfort other than that derived from memories. Memories of her serene face gazing at me with pride. She had known me as a boy alive with energy and a young man who would visit, help and adore her.

As I sit in my chair, I am thinking of her now as if she is looking down on me. I have changed so much from what she would remember. I am old, embittered and alone. The front door bell rings; I remain in my seat – I don't answer the door these days.

But, just a few moments ago, I saw a face – undoubtedly my mother looking down at me. It was not her peaceful, serene face. It was a face full of pain, looking at the man I had become. She had on her face a look of shock. I looked up at her and her pain became mine. Slowly that face disappeared; I was glad it had gone. I continued to sit, thinking. It had never occurred to me to think of how my mother would have remembered me. Not as I am at present certainly; she would never have thought of that. I can understand why she would be horrified at that.

My phone rang – a text, not a call.

I rarely answered the phone but I looked at texts. I pulled my phone out of my pocket with knarled arthritic hands and looked at the text – from a number I did not recognise.

It said: 'I still love you; please believe me, I do still love you.'

The Firework Display

Black skies. Pouring rain. Of course it was. He had set up firework displays in the dry – even in the sunshine – but such occasions were rare. It was, after all, an English winter.

He grabbed his rain coat – and the phone rang.

The landline. So it was Dick. Dick was the manager of Starry Night Fireworks, and was the only member of the company who did not use a mobile phone.

If it was Dick, that was bad news. It usually meant a client was making a late change in arrangements; the wind direction had necessitated a change in the orientation of the site; there had been a problem in supply…

He answered the phone.

'Stuart!' Dick did not speak on the telephone – he bellowed.

'Something I'd like you to do for me.'

Stuart waited with a feeling of apprehension.

'Not a problem,' but then it never was, even if it was a problem.

'I need you,' his boss said, 'to take someone along with you.'

Indeed, it was not a problem. Company on the ride. Help with what had been planned as a one man show.

'My son.'

'Peter,' Stuart said, 'but…'

'Yes, he's young. But I want him to get into the feel of displays. I want him to follow in his father's footsteps.'

It could be worse.

'What does he know?' asked Stuart.

'He doesn't know anything. He's a bit wet behind the ears.'

'Well, he'll be wet everywhere else today,' Stuart said, staring at the pouring rain.

Dick, as usual, ignored the joke.

Stuart drove to the 'factory' of Starry Night Fireworks and started to load his van. 'Factory' was a misnomer; the company made only a few fireworks; mostly the items that left the premises were bought in 'units', being assembled into barrages, bouquets, and other composite items. Even the huge cone-shaped, volcano fireworks were fixed to pieces of 'two by two timber' with fountains linked to eject fire, lava and sparks around them.

He inspected the mortars – as usual the last users had not cleaned them out after their show, so his first task was to remove the many bits of paper and cardboard debris, in some cases large remains of mine lift-charge casings.

At this point, Peter arrived with his father and, as Stuart's boss left, he realised that the young man might be of some benefit after all.

On being instructed to continue cleaning out the mortars, Peter asked:

'What do these do?'

Stuart looked up, wondering if Peter were joking.

He was not.

'Well, they don't *do* anything. You fire shells or mines out of them.'

'Oh, I don't really know about shells; I've only seen one firework display – my Dad took me – and there were only some giant rockets and things.'

'No rockets.'

'But they burst in the sky – lovely big flower-like shapes.'

'But they weren't rockets; this company hasn't used rockets

for – what – twenty years. Shortly after I started work here. Big plastic things with metal motors and long wooden sticks. They were too likely to land in the audience.'

'So shells are safer?'

'For the audience.'

'Aren't they safe for the "operator"?' Peter questioned, rather proud of his use of the word 'operator'.

'A lot safer than they used to be.'

Peter looked puzzled.

'We load up shells in racks, connect them to the electric igniters, cover them over – and fire them remotely.'

'And before?'

'The "loader" dropped a shell in each mortar and moved on to the next rack. After all those shells were fired by the "operator"' – Stuart said smiling – 'the "loader" would come back and fill all the mortars again. You're clearing out the mortars, so you know how much debris is left behind – well, after firing, that debris is likely still to be burning.'

'But they were "fired" remotely?'

'No, no, they were lit by portfire. The "operator" lit a long burning firework like a smouldering fountain and, with it, lit the fuse which came from the bottom of the shell, wound round to the top and then up, and out of the mortar. And the fuses weren't that long in their burning time!'

Stuart pointed at the mortars.

'You'll need to work while we talk.'

'And so the fire travels along the fuse and to the bottom of the shell?' Peter asked, ignoring the instruction.

'It lights the gunpowder lift charge at the base of the shell, which propels it out of the mortar, in turn igniting a time delay fuse which burns for 3 or 4 seconds to ignite the burst charge in the middle of the shell. This distributes the "stars" in the flower patterns you saw.'

'So a shell can never be a rocket?'

'Unless,' said Stuart, 'it's a shell-headed rocket, but we

won't go into that. They aren't used in our – in any – displays now. We can continue the education on site.'

The van loaded, Stuart then explained why he, with the appropriate licence, was, of the two of them, the only one able to drive it. Peter looked at the map.

'It's a small show,' Stuart told him. 'Just two thousand pounds – that's why I was designated to do it on my own.'

'And now you have my help,' Peter said, apparently unaware that he was likely – with his lack of knowledge of fireworks – to be more of a hindrance.

The rain continued to fall heavily. Stuart quickly disabused his fellow operator of the idea that the show might be postponed by the company.

'Once the display is cleared by Starry Night, the client is the boss. I've been left waiting about on occasions for the client to make up his or her mind. But, at a certain point, we have to say – we go ahead or you pay. That makes up their mind. And that won't happen today. I know the client; he'll go ahead in any conditions if the wind's in the right direction and if there's no thunderstorm.'

'Electricity,' Peter said.

'Quite, lightning strikes are a major risk to the electrically fired fireworks and the operators – now start carrying the mortars up to the back of the site and start staking them in.'

Peter looked pained.

'And you can take two at a time,' Stuart said, ignoring his obvious reluctance.

Stuart took out the site plan with numbers on it which corresponded with the numbers of each firework, and began to lay them out.

When Peter returned for more mortars, Stuart told him that the fireworks had had to be covered in the past but that now they were sealed in polythene so that rain could not penetrate.

What it did penetrate was his shoes, shirt and trousers.

But, after an hour of discomfort, the sun shone through.

'So how do you light them?' Peter queried.

'Through the polythene covering. But that was not always the case – in fact that's a recent development.'

Peter mumbled as though his interest in display work were waning.

'I well remember,' Stuart continued, ignoring Peter's lack of enthusiasm, 'a day when the weather was fine, and the forecast was good. I ploughed on without covering the fireworks. Then there was a cloudburst. It only lasted minutes but everything was saturated. The fuses – Chinese fuses in particular were poor then – were sodden, useless. It took another hour to pull them out and to put in igniter cord – a waterproof plastic fuse. And *then* I covered them and had to rush on to complete setting up.'

'So, you've had problems?' said Peter.

'There are always problems. You have to be prepared. One year the truck was loaded for me and the show was mostly shells. But someone had forgotten to load up the mortars and I, stupidly, didn't check before we left.

'Well, by this time, we were about a hundred miles from base. I tried local firework companies – who were willing to help but didn't have all the right sized mortars. Eventually a small display operator supplied most of what we needed, although some were a tighter fit for the shells than we required. I tried an old trick and got one of my colleagues to go out and buy some Vaseline which I rubbed on the shells to smooth their exit,'

'Did that work?'

'Well, some of my colleagues were sceptical but, for the few that were in tight mortars, it worked. But the use of Vaseline is a practice not to be recommended – shells come out with a lot of power – which is why you should never put your head over a mortar.'

Peter looked on but Stuart, seeing that not all the mortars had been moved, decided that his recollections of the old days would have to wait. The mortars had metal loops through which iron bars were pushed and hammered down into the ground. For those racks missing loops, four angle irons were secured at each corner.

Peter was detailed to collect the numbered fireworks – in order – from the van.

'Look for cakes,' Stuart said.

While he expected his young assistant to make a joke about this, it appeared that he had as little sense of humour as his father. Stuart felt pleased – he had heard the jokes so many times before.

'Cakes are oriental barrages or batteries containing a large number of firework tubes with a single fuse running through the base of each tube.'

Peter's definition surprised Stuart:

'Did your dad tell you that?'

'No, I do have some firework knowledge you know.'

It was said in a haughty fashion, which, despite the amusement it generated in Stuart, annoyed him too.

After nearly an hour in which Stuart erected a set-piece, Peter had been staking cakes, placing them on tiles as instructed – so that no damp could penetrate the bottom of the firework.

Peter questioned the practice:

'If the fireworks are weather-proof, why is that necessary?'

Stuart's annoyance was increasing:

'Belt and braces,' he answered. 'Besides which it will improve the chances of the firework not falling over.'

Then he looked at the stakes that Peter had inserted to give the cakes, particularly the taller ones, greater stability.

'You do know things, Peter,' he said, 'but what would happen if that barrage fell over?'

'It won't, you said…'

'If it did?'

'Well, it would just fall over.'

'Where?'

'On the ground.'

'Yes, but it is shooting big stars; where is it now shooting them?'

'Towards, ah, yes, towards the audience.'

Stuart nodded and smiled as Peter pulled out the stakes and re-located them on the audience side of the fireworks.

'Then tape them to the stakes.'

This operation complete, Stuart handed his young assistant a spade:

'We need holes for the posts which will support these set pieces,' he said.

Four hours after they had begun work, Start demonstrated how the firework fuses were secured to the bell wiring which led to the 'slave' and on to the main firing box.

'I thought it was all done by computer?'

Stuart smiled: 'You get that if you pay big bucks. This display gets fired manually, not automatically by computer.'

He separated the two plastic covered wires from the bell wire, securing one strand to a firework and the other to the next one.

'So,' said Peter, 'the wires run from one firework to the next. Are they all joined?'

'No, there are a number of separate firing circuits. When the first batch of shells are over, we'll fire the candle bouquets.'

'Roman candles?'

'Yes, and then a row of cakes.'

'Then the wheels?'

'Yes.'

'And then…'

'Look at the plan.'

Having studied the plan, Peter began wiring.

'What was it like using portfires? Were you scared?'

'No, I loved it.'

'You *loved* it?'

'Fireworks going off all around me, it was brilliant. It is the

147

thing I miss most about the old days.'

Peter was clearly glad that any involvement he would have with displays would be with modern safety measures in place.

'Have you always done displays on your own?'

'No, I don't do all of them on my own – only the smaller ones. And, before I joined Starry Night, I used to organise my own displays – buy them, set them up and fire them. I sometimes had help – usually not very helpful help.

'Once I had a "team" assisting. I went off to get some more fireworks and, when I returned, the "team" had arranged the candles in a semi-circle surrounding the area where the front of the audience would be.'

'Oh, not good.' Peter seemed to be picking things up.

'Certainly not if you were in the line of fire of the outer fireworks, which were pointed straight at you. Needless to say, I quickly got them to line them up – but the person whose idea it was was still explaining why his idea would have produced a much more interesting display.'

The wind – that enemy of the fireworker – had picked up; the sky threatened more rain. Stuart's feet were wet from the earlier deluge but, having put on his fireproof overalls, he was ready to start the display. A final check on the wind direction revealed it to be - as forecast, and according to the display planning – upwind of the audience. The final task before firing was a last check on the firing circuits.

This final check was normal procedure and, although the checks carried out earlier in the day had often failed, and alterations made, the last one was crucial but had never before provided a problem.

Stuart did three tests before each display. This time he turned the wheel to each of the first seven numbers and found seven of the ten circuits returned the required green light. The next three did not. The time set for the display to start was seven o'clock – he had five minutes to discover the issue and resolve it.

To Stuart's surprise, Peter, having struggled into his overalls, was quick to follow Stuart to the fireworks on those three circuits. And he readily pulled out a strong torch.

'Shine it down here.'

As Peter did so, he identified the problem.

'Broken wires.'

He pulled out electrical tape to bind them together and they followed the wire along the fireworks where multiple breaks were identified on each of the three circuits.

Once all were secured, Stuart tested the three circuits on the box. The green light shone as each was tested and – to be safe – he re-tested the other seven.

'Rats or squirrels,' Peter said.

Stuart, while turning the key to 'on' for the first sequence, looked at Peter:

'You did well.'

Stuart's displays always started with a sequence unique to Starry Night Fireworks. The reason for this was that the whistles and strobes used in it were the best available – and now the only fireworks manufactured by the company. Their loudness and brightness were Starry Night's trade mark and encouraged many event organisers to employ the firm. Stuart remembered their introduction and what he had been told by the reporter on the local paper:

'I arrived and talked to a few people and then I was leaving – as I do every year – to file the report I wrote last year, with a few small amendments. But, as I was on my way out, I heard and saw those fireworks – staggering.'

'So you came back?'

'And watched the whole show!'

Stuart began the candle sequence, a row of cakes and the first shells. If Peter had been correct as to the reason for the wires being broken – he had apparently noticed bite marks in the plastic covering the wires – the offending animals had obviously not returned once the action had begun.

The mines, too, were special to Starry Night, ejecting stars, crackers, croakers – anything the staff could find to enliven their performance.

The wheels set piece worked perfectly and the cones-and-candles were sufficiently impressive to evoke applause.

As the final – 125mm – shell sequence ended and the Goodnight lancework set-piece marked the end of the display, the crowd erupted:

'Go on and get your applause.'

Peter hesitated:

'Me?'

'You saved the display,' Stuart told him – not with complete accuracy.

Peter, although he was probably invisible to the enthusiastic audience, bowed – and laughed.

Stuart could remember, in earlier days, walking towards the audience and making circle-patterns of fire with his last portfire. The euphoria prompted him to remember how his love of fireworks started – the huge cabinets in shops, full of every imaginable type of British-made firework – the small tubes which were crimped and waxed and sold with the wax still joining several fireworks together. The jumping crackers, the Catherine wheels, the… And Guy Fawkes' Night, when the sizzling of the first touch paper heralded a night of enchantment.

Peter would never know that world of magic, but he would do alright. Stuart looked at him and his face – shining with joy. He would never even know the pleasure of portfire-fired displays and the surge of emotions that they produced.

But Peter, like Stuart, would eventually be known as the firework man and – like Stuart - he would experience what Stuart believed to be one of the best feelings in the world.

I Knew You Would Come

The gusting wind threw rain against the windows like handfuls of pebbles. He donned his coat; he had to go out. He knew he was being foolish, but could not resist the compelling drive to do so.

Hood fastened, he looked up at the blackening sky and made his way to the seafront. Still at the back of his mind was the nagging feeling that he should not see her. What was there to gain by seeing her? But he was driven: he would see her.

There was something furtive about his progress – and the way he slowly ventured forward: he scanned the seafront. His mobile phone rang. Even at a time like this he worried that his phone would be soaked as he swiped the screen. It was the same number; he had no desire to add the number to his contacts – but then he had no name to apply to it. The same voice that he had heard so many times during the preceding weeks issued from his phone. He lifted it to his ear.

'I knew you would come,' it said.

'Who are you?'

As usual the voice ceased; the rain ran up his sleeves – the wind nearly taking the phone from his hand.

She knew he was there; she knew he would come.

He looked at the wet seats; there was no alternative to walking backwards and forwards. Would she show herself?

As he had done so many times before, he pressed the phone symbol and tapped the number of the last caller– the number which appeared repeatedly on his list of recent calls. He had his reasons for not blocking the number; too often his dreams had been punctuated by unsettling recollections. And he was determined to know who this woman was and why she was tormenting him.

He held the phone to his ear: 'Where are you? Who are you?' he asked – those questions asked so many times in recent weeks.

But this time there was a reply: for the first time she had spoken in response to his call.

'Go into the shelter.'

'Which shelter; which one?'

She was no longer on the line but the question was unnecessary. She knew where he was and that there was only one seafront shelter nearby. As he entered the shelter he was protected from the wind and rain for the first time since he had left the house. But there was no comfort in that. There was no one in the shelter. He peered out of the windows but the severity of the weather prevented him from seeing out. He went to the opening on the sea side; he saw no one.

He had started to receive her calls three weeks ago. At first he had ignored them: one received so many calls, emails, texts which could be deleted. But the calls were daily and sometimes hourly. He should have ignored them, hung up and... but there was some imperative which held his brain in thrall. He stared out at the raging sea, at the sheets of rain. It was hardly surprising that he was alone on the seafront; not even the dog walkers had braved this weather. But he was not alone. He knew she was out there. He accepted that she knew where he was.

The waiting frightened and angered him. How could she control him like this? The rain ran down his coat, down his collar and also from his hair into his eyes. What did she want? After half an hour of waiting, he left the shelter and looked to the west, to the east, across the road – and even out to sea. He did not rule out anything.

But, finally, he shrugged. He would end it. He walked back

along the path to his house, changed his clothes on arrival and took out his phone, tapping the 'settings' button. He blocked the number from which she had rung. He sat down, feeling a sense of relief.

The landline rang.

He picked up the phone but did not speak:

'Did you really think you would get rid of me as easily as that?'

She must have tried his mobile again and received the message that he would not receive her calls.

'Alright,' he said, 'you have my number; I'm in the directory. You probably have my email address as well.' (She laughed). 'But tell me what you want and let's get it over with.'

'Oh, I have time,' she said, 'plenty of time.'

But he was determined to continue his normal life. It was a more serious matter, now, he accepted, but it must not ruin his life. Was it a scam to do him out of money? He did not think so. He had checked his bank accounts and credit card statements: no unauthorised transactions had been made. He did not think she knew his personal details. But he did not rule that out.

If she did not previously know where he lived, she need only to have followed him to discover his address – but he was convinced she knew that already.

He put on the kettle and went to the front door to take in the milk. He opened the door and, as he did so, he caught a flash of something. Of a person? Was he imagining that? He ran out into the garden and looked all around, up and down the road. There was no one to be seen. But then he turned back; if there had been someone, could she have hidden behind the bush and entered the house through the open front door? He looked back, walked to the door but collected the milk from its box on the doorstep to retain a sense of normality. Should he check the house? Was he becoming paranoid? Perhaps he had reason.

He looked to right and left as he entered the house, took the milk through to the kitchen.

No more calls were received on his mobile phone. And, if she knew his email address, she never used it. After two days he had heard nothing, but he did not relax. Her presence was always hanging over him like the sword of Damocles and his work was suffering; he knew he was becoming irritable and bad tempered – even with his best friends. No, his life had not always been stress-free: there could well be reasons why someone would seek revenge on him. Could that be the reason someone was taunting him, upsetting his life? He sat in his chair and opened a book: he must be calm. She was succeeding if she just meant to scare him, spoil his life.

Then the phone rang. It could be anyone, a cold call, a friend, a relative. But he knew it would not be. It was not. She said only: 'I am here; things will start to happen.' He did not reply.

He sat again and opened his book. But he could not read. He put it down and walked into the kitchen. Having made a cup of tea, he brought it to his chair. It was not surprising that he fell asleep. He was not sleeping at night. But the sleep brought no relief: he dreamed that he was walking along and that a woman was tailing him, creeping from bush to bush to bush, from tree to tree. She carried a long knife. It also brought the sounds of screeching car tyres, of the impact when his car smashed into the side of the car which had appeared out of the gloom. It brought back the pictures in the newspaper of the accident, of the woman who had survived (although suffering serious head injuries) – and her daughter who had not survived. He did not need reminding that he had taken no further action, that he might have been to blame and that he had never taken the risk of prosecution by admitting his part in the tragedy.

He awoke with a start; his tea was cold. He sat there staring at the phone.

Going out did not relieve his mood. He was constantly on the lookout. Even in crowds he was careful not to brush against people, not to give an opportunity...

Life continued; occasionally the phone would ring and startle him. But it was never the voice that he most feared.

As he set off for work, he was careful – when catching the train – not to stand too near the platform's edge. And, when he returned each night, he was beginning to avoid the eyes of neighbours. As, one evening, he put his key into the lock, it did not turn as usual. He could not have failed to double lock it. He always...

He eventually managed to turn the key and pushed the door open. The door had not been double locked but it still would not be possible to push the door open without a key. Nevertheless he opened every door inside the house tentatively. The downstairs toilet, the lounge... after all he had never quite understood how his window cleaner was able to unlock three bolts down the sideway to wash the back windows. From there into the house by the back door would have been easy for *him*. He walked through the kitchen to the back door.

It was unlocked. If he went into the back garden, he did sometimes fail to lock it again. But surely...?

He opened the door under the stairs and peered into the gloom before flicking on the light: there was no one hiding there. He mounted the stairs, looking ever upwards until he reached the landing; opened the bathroom door... the bedroom door. He tore open the wardrobe door and then gave a sigh of relief. There was no one in the house. Then, on returning to the landing, he looked up at the loft hatch. It was not how he normally left it.

It had not quite clicked flush with the hatch opening. He might have accidentally left it like that of course...

But he could not leave it. He had to check the loft. How could he sleep (not that he had slept much since the calls had begun) knowing he had not checked the loft above him, knowing that, at any time during the night...?

He walked downstairs to get the ladder by which he normally climbed into the loft. He opened it up with trembling hands and set it against the side of the hatch.

As he climbed the ladder he realised how vulnerable he was to attack from above. But it had to be done. When he had reached the top he flung back the hatch and flicked on the light.

There was no one in the loft and nothing to indicate that anything in it had been moved.

He felt a little calmer; for the moment he knew that there was no one in the house.

But he needed to go out; he had to go to work, to get provisions. And, when he did so, he dreaded what would greet his return. He was more than ever convinced that, at times, he had not been alone in the house.

On his return, he opened the door. Had he left the books he saw, lying on the floor? He knew he had put them on the table. Things in the hall, too, had been disturbed. His coats from the coat stand were on the floor. Not only had someone been in the house but, for the first time, that person had not hidden her presence. He sat on the bottom step of the stairs to summon courage to search the house. He checked the downstairs toilet. It had obviously not been entered. He moved on and opened the door to the lounge.

He could see, some way from the door, in front of his settee, a dark shape: a mound that could be none other than a person. If this was his persecutor, she was surely not about to leap or strike. She was not a threat to him. He thought she was dead. The way she was lying suggested that he was looking at a dead body.

There was no question that someone had entered the house, but why had they not been seen? Then he thought of the number of times he had seen strangers enter the house next door. He had never questioned their right to do so. Then another question occurred to him. Had his persecutor sufficient spite to commit suicide in his lounge? It seemed absurd but he did not know the limits of her hatred.

He quickly shut the lounge door. He had no wish to view the body. And, with a remarkable awareness given the circumstances, he determined to go nowhere near the body, where subsequent checking could have proved his presence. He used the upstairs phone to call the police.

There was surprisingly little time between his call and a

ring on the doorbell. An officer flicked his identity card and entered with a female police officer.

'In there,' he said to the male officer, who quickly stepped ahead of him.

He watched from the front door, and could just see the policeman touching what, he was now convinced, was a corpse.

He waited while more officers were called, while men in white coats entered the house. Absurdly, he wondered whether they were making any marks on the carpet. It seemed like hours until he saw the stretcher being carried out of the door and into a waiting ambulance. During this time he had moved to a chair in the conservatory, sitting with his head in his hands.

Would you please come to the police station? Yes, of course. He sat in the back of a police car, somehow worried that the female police officer had gently pushed his head down while he had entered it. Could it be that he would be blamed for...? Was he a suspect? The body had been found in his house. Of course he would be a suspect. His heart was beating faster.

He sat in a small room. All the procedures that he had witnessed in police dramas on the television were carried out. His finger prints were taken, his DNA determined by the taking of a mouth swab; swabs were also taken of the skin surface of his hands and arms, and the contents of his pockets were emptied out. He endured the taking of a number of photographs, although the interviewer showed surprising kindness.

He had been invited to view the face of the woman from the lounge. Did he know her?

'I have never seen her before in my life,' he said.

Did he not know her at all?

Well, he thought she might have been...

The story of the phone calls, the day on the seafront: it all came out.

'But, if she had entered your house to kill you...'

'No, no, I don't know why, how...'

157

Could it be that they thought his story an invention?

Had he ever lost his mobile phone?

Well yes, about a month ago, but he had recovered it.

'But it had been out of your hands for how long?'

'A day or two; I was on the point of reporting it stolen when it was returned to me, left in my garage with a note posted through the door. I thought that was kind of someone, but it wasn't signed.'

'May we please see the phone, sir?'

He handed it over. Another police officer turned it on. He spoke:

'The lady in your house had a mobile phone in the pocket of her coat. It may not have been hers; we can't tell, but, given what you tell us about the phone calls, that is not surprising.' He tapped the phone icon and scrolled down. 'The phone's number is listed many times on *your* phone.' He tapped the settings button, then 'blocked numbers'.

'I see you had blocked her number?'

'Yes, yes, I did and I didn't get a call from her after that – only on the landline.'

'And you are in the phone directory?'

'Yes.'

'And she could easily have looked up the landline number – and it appears from what you say that she had found out where you lived.'

'I suppose so, yes.'

'Well, that explains a lot; thank you.'

He leant back in his chair with a feeling of relief.

'But it doesn't explain how, if she entered your house bent on murder, she ended up dead in your lounge, murdered?'

'No, no: was it murder?'

'It was murder and, if she was trying to kill you, there might be a case for self-defence?'

'I didn't kill her; I didn't touch her; I didn't go near her.' He collapsed on the desk and wept.

He expected, and received, more difficult questioning from the police. He sat in a number of small rooms, answering the same questions, feeling more and more tired. While an air of politeness persisted, he was aware of a more forceful approach. He was brought tea (which he could not drink) but he was intimidated by the harsh looks on the faces of those (he realised more senior officers) who took up his interrogation. The word had not occurred to him before: this was no longer a friendly chat; it was interrogation and he was careful not to answer carelessly. He was innocent; he had no reason to fear but the circumstances, he realised, pointed to him as a murderer.

'Thank goodness I didn't touch her,' he thought. 'So there was no proof that I had ever been near her.'

The kind policeman had told him, when he was first brought in, that there was no DNA on her body which connected her with him. Sometimes the fact that someone had been in a room – (which he had every day of his adult life) – meant that DNA attached to a body. But in this case there was no sign of any emanating from him. He was grateful for that explanation – although he realised the policeman probably should not have told him.

He was released although he knew he was not free from police investigation. He sat at home and took up his book. He would always be haunted by the experience and by the mystery of how the perpetrator of this mystery had ended up, dead, in his lounge. He could try to explain it but he could not convince himself.

He must put his life back together.

The phone rang. For the first time for some time he strode to the telephone without fear.

A familiar voice answered:

'I thought you would touch her, want to see the face of your tormentor; anyone else would. I succeeded in one thing. She is dead, the bitch. Getting the two of you would have worked so well together; it's a pity. But this time I will get *you too*.'

For some time she waited; he could not speak.

Then she laughed that horrible laugh:
'You are not safe!'

The Girl Who Was a Crocus

'I haven't much time. I have to go soon,' Iris said. She looked at him in a nervous way and walked towards the door.

'But wouldn't you like to stay, Iris, just for a moment?'

He took her groceries from the counter and wrapped them.

'No need to leave,' he said. 'I'll get you some string for these.'

As he left, Iris picked up her groceries and sidled towards the door. Then, feeling like a child caught in the act, she remained with her hand on the door handle as he returned.

'Just a few goes with this, Iris,' he said, apparently not noticing her move towards the door.

'But it's just round the corner…'

The assistant took the bundle from her and replaced it on the counter, winding string around it.

'I could have had a bag,' she said.

'No, no. With the weight of the groceries, they would have been in the gutter before you'd got them a hundred yards.'

The shop doorbell clanged as another customer entered.

'That should be it – nearly,' he said. 'Just one more little piece of string after I've served this lady.'

'But really – it's alright now. I can manage,' Iris said.

But the assistant was already attending to the newcomer. Iris stood impatiently, watching the flashes made by reflections of the sun on passing cars and listening to the steady hum of the traffic making its way coastward.

She watched the customer leave. The assistant had gone in search of more string.

'That's what I should have had,' she said.

'What should you have had, Iris?' asked the assistant, returning with an even larger ball of string.

'A shopping bag. It would save all this wrapping up and I should have got home sooner.'

'But I like to wrap your things for you Iris. I like to give personal service in the shop – I pride myself on the personal service we give.'

Iris took the parcel. The assistant smiled and held open the door.

'Good day, Iris,' he said.

She smiled, clutched at her parcel and walked out.

For most of Mervyn Skye's twenty three years, he had been in love. And, while he had had to modify his attentions to Iris Beacham to suit the situation of her marriage to a comparatively wealthy optician named David Lanche-Batford, he had never considered her completely lost. He liked to think, too, that the old feeling that Iris had for him had never died, even when she had started making more visits to the optician's than could be justified by a careful observation of possible deterioration in her perfect eyesight.

When Gabriella had forsaken him for the owner of a sports car and Michelle for a milkman (the latter had seriously dented his pride) Mervyn started to bestow all the old attentions on his first love.

And as he stacked tins or priced jars of chutney his thoughts would return to the rose tinted days of their teens. And, as if to accentuate the nostalgia of the moment, the sun blazed through the shop windows and toyed with the dust which danced in its beams.

The bells of St Martin's were peeling, and Mervyn had to pull himself away from a daydream in which he was leading his erstwhile love down the aisle from the altar at which they had been joined till death did them part.

For the bell which had jolted him had come not from the church but from the door and a man was leaning on the counter, brushing badly aimed confetti from his suit.

The man spoke:

'Very pretty sight,' he said.

'The bride?'

'Gabriella. She'll be eaten tonight.'

Mervyn looked up with a start.

'Gab…?'

The wedding guest laughed:

'Never mind old chap,' he said, nudging the assistant. 'Plenty more fish in the sea. No sense in looking back. And when they've been married a while they begin to regret what they've given up, don't they?'

And suddenly Mervyn was thinking not of Gabriella but of Iris, and wondering whether she was thinking of the past and whether she might return to enjoy the delights of their past. A few seconds later the ringing of the doorbell interrupted his musings and he looked up at the door. At a very familiar figure.

Mervyn collected a few items from the shelves and placed them before the man who, instead of taking them, looked at Mervyn for a few moments with a look which Mervyn felt to be one of appraisal.

'I was told to be careful,' said the man.

'Careful?'

'Careful lest someone stole my wife. I think most people felt I should deserve to lose her.'

Ignoring the items Mervyn had selected for him, the customer made his way to the door.

'Dave, your shopping,' Mervyn called after him. The man laughed, returned to pick up his purchases, and walked out of the shop.

As Mervyn looked down at Iris, he thought of the crocuses she had brought him when they had first met. For some reason, he could not rid himself of the idea that she looked like that flower, and when he told her she had laughed – but had put her arms around his neck and hugged him tightly.

The sun cast a lacework pattern over the bed and puffs of wind rattled the windows, bringing the smell of the morning into the room. Traffic on the main road buzzed by at intervals and threw dark shadows against the far wall. Her eyes half closed and she whispered:

'I think I really am a crocus.'

'You are,' he smiled, 'a crocus in bud ready to open up and look for the sun.'

And the hum of traffic and the clattering window went unnoticed.

The girl slept. Mervyn grasped the phone before its ringing awoke her. He wondered where she had been during the evening that she had returned to him so late. He had not wondered why she had returned to him rather than returning home. He had begun to make certain assumptions about Iris.

He opened a window with one hand while lifting the phone to his ear.

'Do you know,' said a voice, 'what your wife did tonight?'

Mervyn looked at Iris, sleeping on the bed. Sleeping off the effects of too much whisky drunk too quickly. He was indeed curious and implied in his answer acceptance of a relationship with the girl that only the caller's error had created.

Not that he was entirely ignorant of his 'wife's' activities that evening. He had heard a great deal from the policeman who had brought Iris to his house. Again, it had become natural to him that she should give his address as her own.

The coarse voice was still chattering in his ear.

'And I got there about eleven – which was late for me to be out mind – but I saw your wife and she gave me a bit of a shock. I must say I didn't dream she was drunk like – not at first. Just high spirited I thought. Not that there's anything terribly wrong with being drunk. I mean there have been one or two occasions when I've – well – a little over the limit you know. Not really drunk – not like your wife. Mind you I...'

Mervyn sat on the side of the bed and looked pityingly at Iris's recumbent form. What had made her behave like that? Would she have done if she had married him?

The voice was insistent.

'Funny, now that was curious. You see I thought I'd better get away. Fairer, like, on her. But you know how it is. You can't avoid hearing certain things and she was saying everything loud like. Well, as I remember it, she said: "I wish you'd call me a crocus, Dave". Now this was something so curious that I felt compelled, absolutely compelled to... well... I'm sure you're wondering how I got your phone number...'

Mervyn put the phone quietly back on its hook and cradled his head in his hands thoughtfully.

Mervyn returned to Iris. He sat on the bed again and watched her childlike face as a dream plucked at her lips.

'Call me a crocus, Dave. It sounds so nice...'

She awoke with a start.

'It's alright, Iris; you were dreaming. I'll just put the kettle on.'

Mervyn turned out the light and flicked on the switch of the bedside lamp. It was Iris's second night with him but the proprietary air he had adopted had gone. He hung his clothes carefully on the back of the chair and pulled back the sheets.

Iris smiled. He took her in his arms and kissed her gently. This, he thought, would be the last time he would make love to a crocus.

No Ordinary Ride

It was a day when, in my mind, I was within the pages of my books of wild romance. The wheels of my bicycle turned with increasing speed; downhill was exhilarating, uphill a challenge. My mind raced in and out of adventures as the car-less lanes spanned ahead. It was too early for the cars which would later populate the lanes and, even then, my route was not one on which I normally encountered much traffic. And my ride would continue for as long as I wished to ride.

There were no irritations until I heard the toiling of an engine behind me. I felt mounting annoyance; this was my road, and the winding lane did not permit the car to pass. With a sigh of impatience, I found a layby into which I could pull, waving my hand at the driver of the car so that it could pass. But what I saw, as the car pulled alongside and I was able to see the driver, blew away my annoyance. Sparkling eyes. A radiant smile. A girl in an orange dress, sun-tanned bare arms and shapely legs.

She waved her thanks, continuing to smile.

I watched her drive up the hill. I pedalled hard but her car turned left at the top of the road. The heroines in my mind now had her face, her hair, her eyes, her sun-kissed arms. I yearned to be her hero. But that would never be. Or so I thought.

It was absurd to follow, perhaps, but I turned left at the top of the road in the vague hope of seeing her again. I did not know this road; it was off my usual route and I did not know where I was going – and cared less. I knew she would be well ahead and rode without any expectation of seeing her car, but I continued to cycle the way she had gone.

My spirits began to flag; they were tinged with disappointment that I should never see her again. Dreams and imagination were futile. What I should give to… Ahead I could see a fairground and I turned into the entrance of the field in the hope that she may have also done so. I had always enjoyed such places and I could no doubt go on the dodgems or in a space ship imagining her to be by my side.

I chained my bike near the entrance. And, as I made my way to the dodgems, I saw… I could not believe my luck: the lady in the orange dress was ahead of me. I increased my speed, surprised that she, too, was walking so quickly. And she turned. Not only did this confirm that the girl I was following was she who had passed me on the road, but it showed me the fear on her face. She looked directly at me and raised her hand in recognition but then indicated with the fingers of both hands a walking motion. Clearly, she believed she was being followed, although neither she nor I knew from which direction danger threatened.

The thought that 'my' lady seemed to be inviting my assistance made my determination to be her knight in shining armour all the greater. And then a man appeared round a stall and, although she turned sharply to avoid him, he had clearly not seen her. The look on his face indicated his uncertainty as he searched. But her reaction told me that he was definitely her pursuer. I continued to rush ahead but did not follow her new path. As I approached the man, I swung towards him, knocking him sideways. I had hoped to floor him but had only hindered his progress, although he further wasted his own time in rounding on me and telling me, in choice language, his opinion of the person who had run into him. I was pleased that he clearly did not consider our collision deliberate on my part. It certainly had gained the girl precious moments and, having exhausted his fury at me, he had lost momentum and hesitated still further. I hurried on, not because I feared the man – with my youthful arrogance I felt I could hold my own in any struggle – but because I wished to further mislead him in his search. I took a course away from where the girl had vanished from my sight in case he should follow *me*, but a look over my shoulder showed me that he had not done so.

And I had a good idea of her likely direction – that she would eventually make for her car, which I had seen in the car park at the far side of the field.

This was adventure. This was what my thirteen-year-old self craved. This romance and – I firmly believed – complicity in the girl's crime. Was my orange dressed lady really a criminal escaping from the results of her crime? Or, was she perhaps the *victim* of a crime from which only I could save her?

'I saw what you did for me,' said a voice.

So involved had I been in my daydreams, I had almost forgotten my purpose. But I had certainly not forgotten the girl – even if I had somewhat lost my sense of direction. It was a surprise to hear her; it was a delight to hear her although I had had no idea she was so close. I had not considered how her voice would sound, but she had spoken to me with a voice so sweet…

'You saved me.'

I relished her attention and gratitude. I could not think what to say, so I just stared – and smiled.

Then she did something of which I had dreamt forlornly following our 'meeting' on the road. She held my hand.

'Quickly, we must go quickly.'

We?

I stumbled along behind her. The sun shone brightly on the stalls and on the rides. I, however, had eyes only for the girl who held my hand.

Had I really made such a difference? Had I saved her? Had I enabled her to escape from a criminal gang? Had I ensured that she would reap the benefits of *her* masterly crime?

We were approaching her car and, with a swift look over her shoulder, she withdrew her hand, ran to the driver's side and, as

I opened the passenger door, pulled me in.

I was to ride with her. That wonderful girl. I was aware – very strongly aware – of her legs as she engaged the clutch, of her arms as she turned the steering wheel and, as we began to speed along the road, of the beauty of her face as she turned towards me:

'I expect you're wondering why I was running away?'

I just looked at her.

'I saw him driving along the road behind me and hoped turning into the fair would confuse him. It almost did. He passed where I had turned into the field but, as I entered the fairground, I could see him turning his car and returning. My hope was that I could still evade him, that he would think he had lost me, and not realise I had turned into the fairground.'

I wondered what the girl would think of me, gazing at her open mouthed. She was probably not aware that it was a look of love, of admiration, of devotion beyond my powers of speech to express, although I hoped she had correctly read my expression.

'You were probably surprised to find me in the fairground?'

I continued to stare; I had not given it a thought.

'Well, even if he had eventually realised what I had done, the fairground was an ideal place, somewhere I could mix in with the crowd. Then I saw him and realised I was still being followed.'

She started the engine.

'I know what you are thinking.'

I wondered if she really knew what I was thinking.

'Why did I get out of the car?'

I managed to nod, although I had not really considered her motives at all.

'Well, I thought he might search the car park he was in and then make straight for the other one – although, when I saw him park and walk around the fair, I realised I had miscalculated.'

She thumped the steering wheel of the elderly car in which we sat and informed me that, in any car chase, she would have been the loser and that 'he' had a Mercedes.

'I was on my way to our house assuming he would have

been out but, after his following me, I should have given up any such idea.'

'*Our* house?'

'He is my husband.'

She must have noted the disappointment on my face:

'Well, not for much longer.'

I raised my eyes to her face.

'He treated me very badly. I was only trying to get into our house to take the last of my possessions.'

My face registered the hatred I felt for a man who could abuse this paragon of all the female virtues.

Stopping for traffic lights, she swung round to show me the top of her right arm which, in my concentration on her left side in the car, I had not previously noticed. It was bruised from the shoulder to near her elbow.

Anger welled within me. That he could…

But she continued to tell me of her escape.

'He had told me what he was going to do to me if I tried to get back to the house to retrieve my belongings. I could not risk his finding me there.'

She turned onto the Morpeth Road: 'I can go back to my mother's, or I could…' Suddenly she stopped. She had remembered my bike at the same time that I had.

'We can drive around for a bit,' she said; 'go back to the fairground and get your bike. You could check that he is no longer there. Then we could put your bike in my boot, and I could take you home.'

I nodded and relaxed into my seat, enjoying the sun and her nearness.

When we arrived back at the fairground, I made the thorough and determined search she had suggested. I convinced myself that her husband had gone and received the reward of her warm praise:

'You have shown such courage in helping me,' she said.

It was late in the evening when, all too soon, she parked her car at the kerb outside my house.

'Should I tell your parents that it was my fault you are so late?'

'They will not be worried,' I said, and then watched as she pulled away.

I was unsure whether I should ever see her again. But she reappeared nightly in my dreams and, during my waking hours, she walked beside me in my imagination.

It was three weeks later when a familiar car drew up outside my house. The curiosity of my parents, with whom I had not subsequently shared my adventure, was considerable when, what my father described as, 'a very attractive young lady' emerged from the car and knocked on the door.

I rushed to the door, but my father arrived first. I considered that it was not only curiosity that gave him wings.

The lady he greeted smiled – as she had smiled when I had first seen her. I imagined that my father would be as susceptible to that smile as I had been.

She told him that I had been a 'hero' and that I had 'saved' her.

Naturally she was invited in and, as my mother put the kettle on, began her story of our meeting. My father looked at me quizzically:

'You never mentioned this?'

I had not mentioned it because it was my secret – and it was a secret which would have grown through the years.

I shrugged.

'I didn't really do anything.'

The girl begged to differ and explained what had transpired since that sunny day. The explanation included news of her divorce, which had now come through. She was, she said, 'free'. She continued:

'I wanted to give your son something,' she said.

Although I delighted in her freedom, I was disappointed in

her explanation of how she planned to use it. She had met another man – who would protect her in future as, she said, 'your son protected me that day'.

I bathed in the glory of her words – and, of course, I was pleased that the abuse she had suffered would be at an end, that her ex-husband, the man who had inflicted such terrible injuries upon her, had received a non-molestation order. I should also, I suppose, have been pleased that she would be able to count on the protection of the new man in her life.

But I was not. All I could do was smile and accept what she had brought for me. It was necessary for us all to go out to her car to view the new bicycle she had bought me, which was of a type I could never normally have dreamed of owning.

I almost hugged it to me but what she gave me afterwards I valued even more. She hugged me and kissed me on the cheek. As she did so, she handed me a card which I slipped into my pocket to read later.

My parents re-entered the house. It was as if, as she drove away, they realised I should like to be alone with my memories. I watched until her car could no longer be seen.

I wheeled my new bike towards the garage. And then I remembered the card she had given me. I assumed it would be a note of thanks, but it was not. It was more official in appearance.

I stared stupidly at an invitation 'to the wedding of...'

I put it swiftly back in my pocket. It was not an invitation which I would be accepting.

Under the Railway Bridge

Sally swung her legs out of bed. The sun shone on her legs and on her golden hair. She looked down, pulled up her nightdress, smiled, and moved her legs - exceptionally pretty legs - in a motion like the waves on the sea. She knew that her legs were attractive and it was a source of pleasure but not of pride: she was what she was, a very pretty girl and a delight to the eye.

She, still smiling at the day, jumped off the bed and took off her nightdress, selecting clothes for the day. It would be sunny again. The lack of cold breezes would mean she would no longer require a coat: only a sleeveless, summery dress showing her creamy arms. She ran her hands down her body and prepared for the day.

Chico was not admired. He was hated and feared. There had never been proof that he had used the knife of which he boasted, but he was capable of it – or so it was believed. The common view was that he was capable of anything evil.

He rarely spoke and few spoke to him, believing that he would resort to violence should the conversation take a turn he did not desire. No one risked it.

It was not known how Chico made a living but he did not lack for anything he wanted. This led to the obvious assumption that his 'wealth' was gained illicitly.

His day started with a scowl, with a flinging open of the front door. On this particular morning, he slammed it shut and

173

took out a leather bag to match his black leathers, sliding onto his motor bike and revving its engine.

Then he saw Sally. He found her a compelling sight. She was walking with a swing, no doubt dictated by the rhythm of the music to which she was listening. She passed by and Chico followed her progress. But Sally was unaware that she was observed.

No woman ventured close to Chico by choice. Not only was there the danger of an attack with a knife: for various other reasons a woman was believed to be unsafe in his company. Chico's bike stirred into life.

The warm, sunny spell continued and Sally could enjoy her walks. Her cares were behind her. When she walked on the pavement, the pathways and the alley ways, she was unaware of any interest in her – although she hoped that there might be some.

Sally attracted attention from most females she met. Unlike most men, women are attracted by beauty in those of their own sex. And, since it was combined with a matching nature, there could be no surprise that she was popular with most of the people she met – and was a girl who had many friends.

Perhaps her assumption – far from arrogance or vanity – that she might be watched was leading her into a lack of awareness of any who might mean her harm. She did not, for instance, notice when she tripped along the pathway leading from the railway bridge, that there was an observer of her actions. Had she been aware of it her movement might not have been so carefree. For its source was an angry, brooding presence – a being who could not witness her beauty with merely pleasure. Who viewed her in the same way a cat might a bird: a despoiler of good.

He followed her as he had followed her before. His desire to hide from her while observing her would have told her, had she been aware of it, that danger threatened – and the sounds of slight movements were ignored. When she returned that day, Chico too was returning on foot. It might even have been that he had followed her, such was the uncanny coincidence in the timings of their walks.

As the fine weather continued, Sally would enjoy her walks, although it was now impossible for her to be unaware of Chico's sullen stares of admiration. Although she ignored them, she was not worried. She knew Chico's reputation but it meant nothing to her. It certainly would not influence her in her choice of walks.

And, although she began to be aware of the measured, surreptitious soft tread during her walks, it did not - initially - concern her, and she did not associate it with Chico. She did not even consider that the steps might be following *her*.

Until one day there was a parting of the hedge beside which she was walking. However, her attention was diverted by an elderly man approaching, who stepped back to let her pass. She looked back at the hedge, behind which she thought she had seen a flash of black clothing, but there was nothing now to be seen – and the man who had passed her had seated himself on one of the seats along the path. She shrugged – it was too easy to be worried by unexplained events.

As a result, summer continued its benign progress and Sally with it. Her destination was often the gardens which had once been part of the estate of a manor house and, before that, an abbey whose stone had been used to create the later building and whose foundations underlay it. Some parts of that earlier construction had even been preserved and, when the manor house was demolished, it was these parts which were retained and preserved. And it is in that deserted location that we discover her, enjoying the early morning sun.

Sally had cast away all that she was carrying, and shaken her golden hair free to ripple in the light breeze. The cool stone of the ruins looked inviting. She lay full length on the cill of what had once been a large, ornate window. She did not dwell on sorrow, decay or the past but pulled her skirt higher so that more of the ice cool stone came into contact with her naked legs.

The sun which had previously cast dark shadows on this

part of the ruins was gradually bathing the area in its yellow heat and the girl's face felt its warm rays. A trickle of sweat made its way between her breasts as she made to sit up and she arched her back to ease its irritation.

The town was waking, but few would find her there. She relaxed back onto the stone and smiled, her eyes closed against the sun. It was a position she maintained and, until a bus passed outside the wall, she slept.

She rose languidly and swung her legs off the cill, collected her thoughts and pulled her bag to her. Her dress returned to its normal level just above the knee and she slowly progressed to the old town, to its Elizabethan houses which she loved, and its small café where she sometimes found refreshment.

She walked down a trackway leading from the road and to a recreation area and a playground. While walking she heard steps behind her. She turned – and the steps stopped. She could see no one. But she was unnerved. It was too early for the boys to start their games of football and for the smaller children to occupy the playground. Sally was grasped by indecision. Ahead was an area of empty greensward where she could expect no help if she needed it – and behind, she knew, was a brooding menace on the narrow path.

She felt panic welling up. She walked back down the path. She did not look round but she could hear footsteps and, as she walked more quickly, so did the sound of footsteps quicken.

She hoped she could reach the entrance to the recreation ground, where the path issued into the old town. There was no let up in the pursuit, nor in her speed. Her chest hurt with the effort of running and she could run no faster. She needed to rest but, not until she had emerged into the old town's protection, would she be able to do so.

At last she reached the road and crossed it without looking. A car approached the narrowing of the road but Sally had found the safety of streets along which people were walking.

She sat on a window ledge and looked back. She thought

she caught a sight of black leather but could not be sure. She walked home along populous streets, and eventually unlocked her front door, looking over her shoulder as she did so.

For two days, Sally did not leave the house. Then she ventured out. She heard no footsteps. This seemed to justify her decision not to report the matter to the police, one made partly because she feared what the pursuer would do if he heard of it, and because she doubted whether her plight would receive serious attention.

But, as she returned, she heard noises behind her; every noise she heard made her fearful. She knew that to react to any sound was foolish. She knew that but it made no difference. She feared the footsteps; she wondered whether she would hear them for years ahead. What would he do? When would he cease to track her? A stalker would considerably concern her but she feared more than being followed. Why would he have run in pursuit of her if nothing more was planned?

She speeded up and, again, heard the footsteps matching her pace. How long could she avoid him? How long before she…? She did continue to go out. She had to go out. She had provisions to buy and things to do. But she did so with great trepidation and was often aware of being followed.

Sally had to walk to the seafront and feared the path by which she must travel if she was to avoid a long walk round the streets. However she would do so tomorrow. She could not let her life be completely ruined by this creature.

As the morning sun greeted her waking, she looked out at it with mixed feelings. Gone was the diaphanous nightdress; gone the summery dress. Although Sally woke to the bright sun, it did not bring the good feeling that it had hitherto engendered in her. She did not swivel off the bed; she wearily stood as if the world were an unwelcoming place – as indeed it was. She had awoken in fear and that remained with her whether she left the house or stayed within it. But planning for the day no longer meant choosing the prettiest dress nor being aware of the happiness of others in her own.

She donned a coat although the brightness of the day did not warrant it. She left the house mechanically and fearfully. She looked up and down the street. She could see no one and began to walk towards the beach path. This was not as foolish as it might have sounded. For the first part of the walk, housing skirted each side; only when she passed under the railway bridge did surrounding housing cease, but then the flats would begin on her left and the nursing home on her right. There were few obvious hiding places.

Nevertheless she approached the path with caution, checking all around. And, when she approached the railway bridge, they started. Those steps. She put her hands to her face and she felt like crying, but no tears came. Her walk became a jog, her jog a run but, as with the day in the old town recreation ground, the steps behind increased their pace. And, despite her fear, she was aware of not only one set of steps but two.

At the railway bridge hands seized her. She shrugged them off but an arm came round her body and she was hauled to the ground. Hands went round her throat and she lay, unable to move. But, then, the pressure on her throat eased and a violent noise assailed her ears.

Now the tears did come. She screamed and looked up – into the face of Chico. But he did not touch her other than by picking up her hand and helping her to a sitting position. She looked into his eyes, her fear evident. His eyes seemed to reassure her. He did not speak but motioned with his hand to where a man's body lay slumped on the ground.

Sally looked back at him and, as realisation began to dawn, she said:

'Is he…?'

Chico shook his head, and held his hands out. Despite herself, she took them and allowed herself to be raised from the ground. She could not prise her eyes away from the body lying on the path but allowed herself to be led under the bridge.

'You were going to…?' Chico queried. He motioned towards the seafront. But she shook her head. She would be unable to meet anyone feeling as she did.

He looked at her neck, made to touch the wheals – but withdrew his hand. Chico instead took her hand and led her back towards her house.

Sally had, for some time, had an idea of who her pursuer was. Now her mind tried to cope with a big change.

'You were not…?'

Chico shook his head again:

'I always tried to protect you,' he said briefly.

'But he…?'

Chico opened the door for her.

'You must come in,' she said.

Chico shook his head and motioned the way they had come. His meaning was as clear as if he had spoken. He had to attend to the man who had assaulted her and who, he hoped, remained under the railway bridge. It was perhaps as well that Chico had been obliged to help Sally and not finish his business with him while his fury was at its height. One thing was clear: he would not have used a knife – he did not possess one, nor any other weapon.

The man was still there but sitting up; Chico dragged him to his feet, and he began to walk unsteadily out of Chico's reach. Although he made as hasty a retreat as his condition allowed, Chico had discovered where he lived and where to find him in the future. He could, for the moment, let him go. But there would be no escape for Sally's persecutor: his life would now not be worth living. The man who had made a misery of Sally's happy life would never attack her – or anyone – again.

Chico looked up the path towards the road in which Sally lived, and where she would, in future, live in safety. Then he turned the other way and walked slowly down to the sea.

The Farmhand

The wind blew up dust from the stony track. The hot sun burned down on the apple picking youth; the cooler evenings seemed a long way off.

'You need a hand with picking?'

The scrawny youth looked down from his perch:

'We got all the help we need, thanks.'

The newcomer's gaze was directed to the youth's sister who emerged from the chicken house carrying eggs. He saw the rounded brown shells. The heat had not worried the hens.

'You keep chickens?'

The youth replied: 'Some, there's no profit in it.'

'Is that what your dad says?'

'Sis says it; Dad don't say much.'

His sister gave him a reproving look and moved towards Handy.

'If you're looking for jobs, we have no jobs. We work hard enough for the money we get, and the food and the money won't go any further.'

Handy watched her hands as she played with the protruding wicker strands of her basket. He said:

'I work hard. I'm known where I come from.'

'Where's that?'

'South of here, near Tonbridge.'

'I haven't heard of you. You may work hard but there's no

work.'

The girl could only be eighteen, brown skinned from the sun, with fair hair bleached a golden colour. Handy still stood, looking at her as if he had nowhere else to go.

'We got no jobs. Down where you come from, they may give you some work. But it's hard here. David, go in and take in those apples.' On a sudden thought she handed him the basket too and the boy walked towards the house.

'It's hard here for us. We've got Dad ill and he doesn't understand our position. He'd hire you. He's used to hiring people. He doesn't understand the times. It's been different these last few years.'

Without her basket she had begun to play with the ribbon of her dress. Handy made to go but then hesitated:

'I suppose you could ask your dad?'

Handy sat on the track and pushed his hat off his brow. He continued:

'He's a burden on you and I'll be another. You don't seem to want a burden like me, I know. But I'll work for no pay.'

'I don't want you, but Dad will want you. He'll see you out of the window and ask me what you wanted. He'll get ratty if he knows I just turned you away. No, it's true, I don't want you.'

Handy's raised eyebrows were a question that he did not express and which remained unanswered. He would see her father. He followed the girl into the house.

The old man sat in a wicker seat. He seemed too old to be the girl's father.

Handy nodded to him and removed his hat.

'Your girl was talking to me about a job. She didn't think you needed help. But I want work and somewhere to stay. I'd work for no pay.'

'We need some hands. Women are no good at economics,' said the old man, chuckling. He leant over to the girl and, his hand to his face, he whispered: 'No jobs; you're right, but we can use him.'

He reached over to Handy and took hold of his arm.

'Of course; we need to know about you. Can't sign you on without knowing something about you. And the authorities you know. They need papers, lots of papers.'

The old man took a clip board and started writing as Handy talked about himself.

The girl's father asked for 'more papers my boy. We need papers. And your bank, we need to know that. To pay your money in, you see.'

Handy nodded, omitting to remind him that there would be no money to pay in, and looked at the girl who stood staring at the sun out of the doorway.

'It's too hot, but it's not going to stay dry; we'll have to get the tools in before it rains.' She looked at Handy.

'He likes you. I suppose you've got a job.'

The old man slowly raised himself and clapped his hand on Handy's shoulder.

'Last one left here a rich man.'

'Picking apples?'

'Orchard's for nothing.' He spat on the floor. 'Opportunities, schemes, that's what's on offer.'

The girl said: 'He'll pick apples while he's here and that won't be long.'

'Long enough to make him a rich man.'

The girl looked at her father and shook her head. She bent down and whispered into his ear:

'No schemes this time. I don't want him to be part of any schemes.' She looked out at the fields and shuddered.

The summer cooled and the tree leaves in the orchard turned brown. There had been apple picking, mowing and odd-jobs but the girl was right. There was no justification for an extra hand. Handy heard no more of any schemes as he was not intended to. He ate his fill, slept in the sun and no one showed any signs of pushing him out. It could have been because of the girl. She had grown used to his company and, although she was always offhand in his presence, she knew that he worked only for his keep and did not tell her father to dismiss him. The autumn showed no signs of becoming cold. Handy intended to stay.

The girl spent much of her time with her father.

He told her: 'We want records; have you asked that boy for records?'

'I haven't asked him for anything; I don't want any more of it. Even if you've got the strength to carry on doing it, which I doubt. I'm not having anything to do with your schemes; I'm not getting documentation this time. Not for him.'

Winter soon came and one morning Handy walked into the kitchen to which the old man had moved his wicker chair. The white haired figure was slumped forward; his hands and face were white. He had been dead for some time. Handy looked for the girl but she was not there. The old man's coat contained little except a few pounds and a letter which he pocketed.

The girl did not return until evening. By then Handy had read the letter. It was addressed to her and was in an envelope marked 'Cylene'. His name was mentioned twice. Among other details, including mention of her father's 'schemes', it said that the girl could use Handy. He was dishonest and indolent – he would be no loss; he was just the man they wanted.

When she did come in, the girl bore her normal resigned look.

'Did you know your old…?' he began.

She knew.

Handy could tell she knew much more. She said:

'You know you are indolent?'

'And dishonest?'

'And dishonest,' she confirmed.

'How did you know…?' began Handy.

'What did you do first? Well, that's what I did too. I searched him.'

'And the scheme your dad talked about?'

'There's no scheme now. There could be no scheme without

Dad.'

Handy sat down.

'Hadn't you better be going?' said the girl.

'No more job?'

'There's no more job without Dad. You can't stay here now.'

'No, no, I…'

'There's less money than when you came.'

'You don't have to support your father now.'

'I'm not thinking about supporting him but how he supported me.'

'And yet you left him sitting here while you…'

He looked at Cylene and said nothing more.

'There are arrangements to make. You'd better go.'

He shrugged – but didn't move. And he had not gone by the morning. The summer was over and cold weather was coming in. She still had work to do. She checked the house. She opened the safe: only she knew how to open the safe.

She did not tell her brother, or Handy, what she had found in the safe. There was less to do in the winter – no apples; no produce other than eggs and these, she knew, had declined in the autumn. But they would continue to sell at the stall which opened onto the road.

She saw Handy infrequently, but she knew he had made his home in the barn.

One morning he came out while she was collecting eggs.

'I suppose I had better go.'

She did not speak. She went inside the house and checked the safe. By now, because she had seen him watching when she opened the safe on the previous occasion, she knew it would be empty and it was as she thought.

When she came out he was still there. She would not turn him away. She had become used to his presence. She liked his being around. He lingered, looking, without trying to hide his feelings, at her face, her bare arms and her long bare legs. He looked again into those pale blue eyes, wrestled on his pack and started to walk away, the way he had arrived that summer's morning. She watched him go. Her feelings went tumbling through her; she could not avoid looking at the sinister humps in the earth. He did not slow but looked over his shoulder, his admiration clear to see – and his look of invitation apparent to her.

She ignored it but continued to watch him until he was a speck on the hill, until he disappeared from view. She steeled herself to his departure and coldly told herself that he was of no use to them now, anyway, without her father.

Cylene went into the house, feeling the cold. She found the document she had earlier removed from the safe, which, under his prying eyes, she had secreted in her dress.

She threw it into the fire; she had no need to make him join those under the mounds around the farm. It made little difference. Her father had left her well provided for, she thought, as she again surveyed the mounds in the field.

She called her brother, but he did not reply. She then heard a siren, and voices: her brother's and other voices. She slipped out of the sideway to the fields and kept under the trees from where she could see what was going on at the farm without herself being seen. She was gaining ground on Handy and, eventually, drew level with him. He gave her a knowing look and took her hand.

He gently transferred his hand to her arm and steered her away from the farm. She knew. Perhaps she had always known.

The Strange Tale of Mr Chaplain

'Just another day. Not much going on, Sarge.'

'But a phone call just came in?'

'Yes, Chaplain called.'

'And…'

'Well, we don't bother too much about Chaplain.'

'We bother about everyone.'

If PC James felt that his sergeant's attitude evidenced a certain amount of hypocrisy, he did not say it:

'Of course we do, Sarge.'

'And Chaplain…?'

'Thinks he's being watched.'

'And is he?'

'How do I know?'

PC James stopped, coughed, and took another tack.'

'He might be, Sarge; he's weird and…'

'In what way weird?'

'Well, he's a recluse.'

'So?'

'And he imagines things.'

'How do you know that?'

'Well he's phoned before.'

'About what?'

'Same thing; people are out to get him.'

'What's happened before?'

'We've been round; he's perfectly alright. We've found no evidence of anyone being in his house – and we *would* I think. We visited the neighbours and they would not even recognise him. He lives in a detached house and that's what he wants to be – detached.'

'Who went round there?'

'Evans, sir.'

'Well, you go round this time.'

'Oh, Sarge.'

'If he sees a different officer, he'll be more satisfied.'

'I doubt it.'

'And we'll get a different perspective on the case.'

'But…'

'We need someone who cares, someone who will do all they can to allay his fears.'

PC James ignored his sergeant's irony and got his coat.

Belgravia Close was one of those roads that befitted its name. It was a short road of select dwellings. And its residents had the forbidding air of those for whom sociability was not a priority.

Number twelve – there were only twelve houses - was at the end of it, some fifty yards from its neighbouring house. But, while others employed gardeners to tend their wide areas of garden, no one had been seen tending the garden at number twelve. Hence there was a wildness about it – not exactly unkemptness but an impression of being little tamed.

PC James decided to talk to neighbours and found them, on the whole, uncaring about the situation of Mr Chaplain at number twelve. He was rarely seen and that was how his neighbours liked it. The man at number ten, despite his comparative nearness, could not supply any more information. He had not seen Mr Chaplain for three weeks.

The question asked at every house where a resident answered its door (and he suspected that some – although in – had not) was whether a stranger had been seen at the house where Mr Chaplain lived. The answer on every occasion was the same. They had seen no one.

PC James tried to take his sergeant's advice to believe Chaplain's fears - but eventually decided there had probably been no intruder, no disturber of his peace and tranquillity. As far as someone like Mr Chaplain can be credited with experiencing tranquillity.

The policeman knocked at the door of number twelve. It took some time for the door to be answered. He did not need to introduce himself since he was in full uniform but, considering Chaplain's reputation, flashed his card to confirm his credentials.

The occupant of the house said nothing, showing wariness – which was expected, and puzzlement – which was not.

But then Mr Chaplain had made two further phone calls since PC Evans had called, without the courtesy of a visit. He was clearly not expecting a response to his latest phone call.

PC James was led into a lounge which indicated the opulence of the house's owner, and sat in a large, well-stuffed chair.

'Now, Mr Chaplain; I have come to help you find your intruder.'

'Intruder?'

'Oh, yes, you didn't say that he had entered the house this time. But he's been around the place, threatening you.'

The man nodded.

'Where has he been lurking, this intrud… this man who has been annoying you?'

'Garden.'

'Oh, he's been in the garden?'

'Yes.'

'Trying doors?'

'Yes.'

'Threatening you?'

'Yes.'

PC James thought that Chaplain was as monosyllabic as his neighbours, but his reticence did not discourage the policeman from pursuing the case.

'Did he have a weapon?'

'Yes.'

'What weapon did he have?'

'Knife.'

'And he threatened you with this knife?'

'Yes, once.'

'Do you think he will come back?'

'Not now.'

'What has happened to make you think he won't come back?'

'I think I frightened him.'

'You *think* you did.'

'Well, I frightened him. I went out into the garden. I threatened *him*.'

'Ah, well, Mr Chaplain, we do advise the public not to approach...'

'Yes, yes, I know... but you remember my phone call?'

'Yes, I took it. You sounded very much afraid. To be honest I'm a little surprised you took the matter into your own hands.'

'So was I. I just couldn't stand it any more.'

'Well, yes; so you don't want our help any more?'

'I will always rely on the police. I will phone again if I need you.'

PC James muttered that he could quite believe that - but he had clearly not been heard.

'You have been very helpful.'

This sounded a little out of character, but PC James was happy to have completed the meeting with such harmony.

But all was not yet quite done.

'You are,' said the house's occupant, 'the first policeman to have called.'

'Er, no, PC Evans called last time.'

'Oh, of course. Of course.'

'You know, chap with black hair and a moustache.'

'Of course, yes; of course I remember him. I'm sorry, this

business has got on my nerves. I don't know what I'm doing or saying sometimes.'

'Understandable, Mr Chaplain,' PC James said as he walked out into the hallway.

'Don't forget, give us a call if you have any more trouble.'

The door slammed behind him.

As PC Evans entered the police station, his colleague appraised him of his meeting with Mr Chaplain.

'Nice chap,' James said.

'Nice chap?'

'Yes, very civil and he didn't want me to call again.'

PC Evans was clearly struggling with this image of a Mr Chaplain who had accepted the situation and done so with courtesy and politeness.

'What's he playing at?'

'Well, nothing. I think he just assumes that nothing more will happen.'

'Hmm. You took the phone call. Did he sound like the sort of man who...?'

'No, come to think of it, he didn't – which means he's got some plan. He's up to something.'

'He certainly is. When I called on him, he was furious that we intended to take no more action.'

'Yes, but then he hadn't threatened the intruder!'

'And I don't think he threatened any intruder. He's planning something and I'd like to know what it is.'

PC James settled behind the desk. Evans, however, was not satisfied to leave it at that:

'Perhaps we should go and see him.'

'What, now?'

'Whenever you're free.'

His colleague sighed and prepared to go out.

'Ready when you are,' he said.

Belgravia Close was bathed in sunshine when the two men

approached number twelve.

'Lovely day,' said Evans.

'Yes, lovely day. Did you arrange this because it meant we could get out in the sun?'

'Not entirely,' he said.

James looked at his colleague:

'Well, what do we do? Wait for him to come out?'

'You'll wait a long time; a hermit's got nothing on him.'

'Won't he be surprised to see me again?'

But James did not need to worry for, at that moment, a man came to the door.

'So, he's come out for us.'

'Yes. Is that the man you spoke to?'

James nodded.

'Well, I have news for you. That's not Mr Chaplain.'

The occupant of number twelve was shutting the door and re-entering the house. Just who he really was we will discover by going through that door and listening in to his conversation with the owner of the house.

'I'm Jack,' he said to him, 'I bear you no ill-will. You just ticked all the boxes.'

Since Mr Chaplain was tied by his hands and feet, he would have been in no position to tick boxes; nor was he in the mood to help anyone, least of all, 'Jack'.

'You look like me,' Jack said smiling. 'And while you absorb that compliment, I will tell you why I singled you out.

'You are my build and, as for your voice – you could even be mistaken for me on the phone. You don't mix with your neighbours; most of them have never even seen you. And you live in a nice big house in acres of grounds. You see I have done my research.'

Mr Chaplain failed to show that he was impressed. However, Jack, untroubled by the other man's lack of response, continued:

'It was only today that I discovered that you had spotted

me. A nuisance that; it led to an uncomfortable moment when the policeman came.'

'They have come before,' said Mr Chaplain, feeling just a glimmer of hope. 'They will realise you are not me.'

'Ah, they have called before – yes, young plod told me that. Another blunder on my part. That could be a problem if it was the same policeman. On the other hand, you look so much like me that a dumb plod probably wouldn't be able to tell the difference – especially if it was a while ago. Was it?'

Mr Chaplain intended to give this man no information.

'Oh, I don't want to do this, Mr Chaplain, I really don't.'

The sight of Jack's knife quickly disabused Mr Chaplain of his intention.

'Month, perhaps a bit less.'

'Ah, well, I will have to be on my guard, and I won't go out of the door for some time. It was silly to do so just now. But I didn't see any plods. If they call again, I can say I'm your brother. I could well be you know. And that would explain why I answered to the name of Mr Chaplain, or at least didn't question the policeman's using it.'

Jack drew up a chair and eased himself into it.

'Perhaps I should tell you,' he said, 'why I have done this.'

Mr Chaplain showed little interest in Jack's motivation.

'Yes, I see you would like to know. Well, I used to be an accountant in a flourishing company I set up myself. A one-man business. But I made a few mistakes. I won't bother you with the details because I can see you want me to be quick. However I paid the price for those mistakes and I became a tenant of one of Her Majesty's penal institutions. That was less of a problem than what happened when I was released.

'I had hurt nobody, just made a few rich people a little less rich. They could survive easily enough. I had physically hurt no one. But, when you hear that there are many people – social workers and suchlike desperate to help ex-cons, you can take it with a pinch of salt. I was destitute and I took to sleeping anywhere I could. Door-

192

ways, under railway arches, in bus shelters. Again I did no one any harm but they continued to persecute me. Police would move me on, passers-by would aim kicks at me; just the looks of contempt I saw were upsetting enough. The only help I got was an organisation that would come round the streets giving me clothes, soup and some food. It wasn't what I should have bought but then, when you *can't* buy anything, you just thank God for kind people like that.

'I stayed on the streets for years, got to know a number of others in my position but I didn't drink and I didn't take to drugs like most of them. I just planned. I searched for somewhere I could live and, thanks to you, Mr Chaplain, it led me to your house – and you.

'Impressed, eh?'

Mr Chaplain was not impressed. He just wrestled with his bonds.

'There is no need to do that. You can tell me when you need the loo – and I will treat you to some food soon. I know you'll like it because you bought it and put it in your store cupboards. I'm afraid there won't be too much fresh food because I won't be able to go to the supermarket for a while – given what you have told me. I'll be housebound for a while but the police will soon lose interest, if they have any – which I doubt. But I can assure you it will be much better than lying on a pavement in the rain.'

Jack rose and went to the window – solidly barred on the outside.

'No rozzers. No problem for now.'

PC James and PC Evans were unsure what to do, and continued to hide themselves outside the house.

'It could be a lodger – or a relative,' Evans said.

'He answered to the name of Chaplain. I suppose his name could have been Chaplain too, but he would have explained that he wasn't *the* Mr Chaplain who'd phoned – he would have got him, or told me where he was. It's funny, I thought he showed a desire to find out more about the matter from *me*. Now you've told me, I'm convinced he *shouldn't* have been in that house.'

PC James and Evans looked at each other.

'So, do we get a search warrant, or take a look around?'

'A search warrant,' said PC Evans, 'will take time and we have a very flimsy reason to justify it.'

The two policemen kept their cover but approached the house, looking in the nearest windows. They could see nothing unusual.

'There are steps – a basement?'

There was a barred window to the basement but it permitted them to see inside.

What they saw increased the urgency. 'Jack' was advancing towards Mr Chaplain with a knife. Unable to enter the premises, they radio'd for help and ran round to the front door.

Jack had grabbed Mr Chaplain's arm and raised his knife.

'I'm sorry, I've grown quite fond of my taciturn prisoner. But you do understand that I cannot let you live, don't you? Of course you will tell me you'll say nothing about my being here, and then the moment my back is turned…'

Suddenly Jack held still. He was staring at Mr Chaplain's wrist.

'Your wrist. No one else could have had a birth mark like that on their wrist; I remember it too well. The only person who has a birth mark like that…' began Jack.

'… is your brother,' Mr Chaplain continued for him.

Jack laid aside his knife and sat down again.

'But, if you're my brother… how is it your name is Chaplain, not Fordyce like mine?'

'It has been Chaplain only recently – as part of my new identity. I changed it in case anyone had heard about me in my days as a street musician. I wanted to make a break after succeeding in my new business: to become someone, and I didn't want any of the players tracking me down.'

Jack had thought the resemblance uncanny; they were by

no means identical twins, but they could – without the keen powers of observation of a PC Evans – have been mistaken for the same man.

'I can't kill my own brother.'

This came as a relief to Mr Chaplain who said:

'My name is Fordyce, Errol Fordyce, and yours,' he said, now convinced, 'is Jack Fordyce.'

'Yes,' said Jack, 'it seems we have found each other and I have found, not only my brother but my new home.'

Not one to relish the prospect of sharing his new home, Errol Fordyce, in the circumstances, felt obliged to do so. Strangely, too, he found himself pleased to have found his long-lost brother.

'It must be…'

'Thirty years since we last met.'

Mr Chaplain (or Errol as we must now call him) thought for a moment before nodding.

Jack smiled: 'It may seem strange that I feel so good about meeting you again – someone I was about to attack.'

'Would you have killed me with that knife?'

'We were never close – although now I feel we will be – but I've never killed anyone and certainly would not have killed you.'

'Even before you discovered you were my brother?'

'Even before then,' said Jack. 'I was in a difficult position because I had to threaten, and I was wondering just what I would do when you realised that there was no way I could carry out my threat.'

Jack rapidly untied his brother's bonds and helped him up the stairs to the lounge – Errol's confinement had left him stiff and sore.

'Well, what are we going to do then?' asked Jack.

'We are going to share this house. I am going to use my influence to get you a good job in my company. I am never going to despise the homeless – and, oh well, we have a long time to think about the future.'

Jack laughed as they settled into comfortable chairs such

as he thought he would never enjoy again: 'I suppose you could resume being Errol Fordyce?'

Errol nodded. It was a long time since his days as a street entertainer.

A shuddering noise could be heard at the front door. The colleagues of the two policemen had arrived. But what they found astonished them.

Jack and Errol Fordyce approached the front door, Jack's arm was around his brother's shoulder in a gesture of fraternal affection that he had never shown during their childhood.

Jack raised a quizzical eyebrow:

'Will you be replacing our front door that you have destroyed for some reason of your own?'

PC Evans sighed:

'This is not going to go down well at the nick,' he said.

How Does It End, Felix?

Felix was a voracious reader. Of all types of book from classics to detective fiction. Although he read e-books, he particularly loved printed books: the pages (which emitted that delightful odour) crinkling in his hands. His favourite picture - which had appeared in early Everyman editions - was that of an elderly gentleman, sitting in his study, entirely engrossed in another world provided by the book in his hand.

And this is how Felix enjoyed reading. He abhorred interruption while the story developed. But there was one type of book which he found troubling – one with an unsatisfactory, an unhappy, ending. Because he lived, while not at the office, in the world of his books – and he liked, as we all do, happiness and contentment – the author who took him on the downward path to tragedy was not one he would choose. Given that he lived through his books, his own 'life' was affected by a hero or heroine who faced the inevitability of regret or sadness. The thought of death at the conclusion of a novel was not one he wished to entertain, nor that of a central character who faced a painful – or possibly ignoble - future.

Modern crime stories, adventures and mysteries were usually safe; he knew that, invariably, the hero would ultimately succeed, however great were the torments and near-death experiences through which he or she must pass. And blurbs could be carefully studied for clues to the endings in other books.

The reluctance to embark upon a tragic tale was symptomatic of Felix's life and nature. He admired the opposite sex while rarely risking rejection, although he felt a safety in falling in love with a beautiful fictional heroine. He worried, though, about delightful heroines whose authors would not allow them a happy ending to their lives.

Thus he had never had a permanent – or even a lasting – relationship with real-life women (or ladies as he preferred to call them). He derived all the romance he needed in his life from his books – among his favourites being those written by a now little read wordsmith named Jeffery Farnol. Felix owned his complete works.

Had Felix embarked on a real-life relationship, he would not necessarily – as he believed – find it unrewarding. But he opted for safety and admired from afar. Thus, his dreams were beautiful, and his imaginings brought to his features a look of happiness and calm. Perhaps this is why, with the effect on his nature of this contentment, he could view the girls with whom he moved through life with not only liking but even admiration. For the strength of such relationships were never tested.

Felix was unable to believe that his own insularity was liable to – and often did – consign those he liked (even loved) to a feeling akin to the sadness which he rarely tolerated in his books.

One book upon which he embarked one sunny morning – a sunny aspect brought about a satisfied mien as he opened the crackling page of the newly purchased volume – had upon its cover a view of the countryside with a gate, as if that gate would open onto a day of delight traversing the green fields of England.

But the story with which it commenced ended in heartache. The boy did not get the girl and Felix felt that she, too, would for ever regret the impulse which took her from the hero's side.

Felix inserted a bookmark and took the book to the shelf in his book cases on which were stored books he never intended to complete or read again.

He wondered whether he should spend the next few minutes selecting another book from his collection – perhaps one he had read and could therefore guarantee the suitability of its ending – or visit the bookshop around the corner. Or download a book to his Kindle. His disappointment would not last long.

But, sitting in his garden, he could see through to the front door along the sideway passage, and, there, was Adeline, with whom he worked and who was the prettiest girl in his office. Perhaps she had the greatest influence on his life by raising his spirits on the rare days when the sun did not shine, and his future seemed bleak. Perhaps on a day when the hero of his book had sped downhill from peace and tranquillity to an unlikely, ignominious, end not indicated by its earlier, more promising, pages.

Yes, he liked her. He liked her very much.

He was unaware of her feelings for him although she was always pleasant – always charming. Not affectionate perhaps but then, of course, work colleagues are rarely affectionate – even when their feelings are stronger than normal.

And her visit surprised him. Felix could not understand why, on a Saturday morning, she was visiting a work colleague.

As he opened the door, she beamed. It was a smile one could only describe as a beam – and it brightened Felix's day even more than the thought of a new book, and crushed the disappointment of the book he had newly consigned to the 'unhappy endings' shelf.

The sun appeared from behind a cloud. Adeline thrust a package into his hand.

'It came at work after you had left on Friday,' she said. 'I thought it might be important.'

Packages frequently arrived after his departure from the office. They were rarely any more, or less, important than packages which arrived at any other time of day. So why had Adeline *really* called? Was there a work matter she wished to discuss? Was she worried about something?

If she were her lovely face did not suggest it. Indeed it suggested radiant happiness which was rapidly communicating itself to Felix.

He took the package and tore it open.

It was not important.

'It's not important,' he said.

'Oh, sorry. I, oh well, I'll be running along.'

'No, please come in and have a cup of tea,' he offered, remembering his manners. After all, the girl had come several miles to deliver the parcel. And, Felix reflected, found out his address. Now, why had she done that?

Adeline nodded.

Felix put on the kettle.

'I was just about to have one,' he said – not entirely truthfully. 'I've been reading; well, I've just, erm, finished a book. Well, not finished exactly.'

Felix found himself explaining to the girl why his reading of the latest book had been aborted. Why had he told her all that? He had never previously told anyone.

Adeline smiled, taking her tea:

'But you miss a lot of good books because of that.'

Felix was not convinced. Life was not like that. The feelings of a lifetime could not easily be dispensed with, even though the attempt to influence him was made by such a pretty girl.

Felix sighed. Adeline realised her attempt had failed.

'Did you know my name came from a novel?'

Felix's interest was aroused.

'And did it end happily?' he asked.

'Oh, yes,' she said 'It was *The Romance of the Forest*. By Ann Radcliffe.'

Felix shrugged. 'Oh, gloomy stuff.'

'Well, yes; she does go through it. But it ends happily. She's OK by the end.'

Felix laughed: 'Ah, well; I'll read that one some time. As you're in it,' he concluded.

Adeline seemed pleased.

'Had you thought,' she said, 'of writing your own book? Then you could ensure a happy ending.'

Felix mused on this thought.

'I can't write,' he said.

'How do you know?' Adeline encouraged. 'You write very nicely worded memos and emails.'

Felix was unsure that carefully worded memos prepared one for a literary career.

'And,' Adeline continued, 'Sir Arthur Conan Doyle didn't know he could write until persuaded to do so.'

This seemed unlikely and Adeline wondered if Felix had read biographies of the creator of Sherlock Holmes which would have disabused him of this quite inaccurate information.

'And Charles Dickens.'

'Charles Dickens? Who persuaded him to write?'

Adeline was unsure of her ground. Perhaps she had gone too far. Felix knew that Dickens' married life had not been as congenial as it might have been. But just because he treated his wife poorly did not imply that, earlier in their married life, she had not set him on the road to literary fame.

'I'm still not sure…' he said.

'Write for me. Write me a book. Write something to please me.'

This delightful thought was more convincing than stories of great writers seeing a light which had led to their embarking on a career which gave us some of the greatest literary masterpieces.

And why did it please Felix so much? Did it say something about his relationship with Adeline? Certainly it did. He was becoming very fond of her. Perhaps he was simply realising just how much he relished her presence in the workplace. Perhaps it had taken her visit to convince him that he was growing to… No, let's not use words like love loosely. If Felix could not find it in himself, even in his mind, to use the world 'love', why did he feel like kissing her? Might he kiss her? No, of course not. But would he write a book just to please her? Yes, he thought he would.

Adeline sipped her tea, showing no desire to leave.

That night, Felix dreamt of Adeline but then embarked on a succession of dreams which, he began to feel, might prove to be the basis of a novel. Perhaps inspired by Adeline, these dreams promised a conclusion sufficiently satisfactory to please Adeline. But, more importantly, to please himself.

Felix's relationship with Adeline was unchanged in the office. At least he felt that no one noticed any change. But then they would have missed Adeline's glances, smiles... even the brushing of a hastily withdrawn hand against his – an action convincingly disguised as mere accidental contact.

And Felix's work on his novel began. Its path followed that of his dreams which seemed conveniently to take a course which directed him to write and which inspired his writing.

After a week Felix had completed thirty pages. As his muse directed, he had commenced a pattern of writing in the early morning before leaving for work, when the inspiration of his dreams was fresh in his mind. In the evening he would type and amend – although little amendment was needed, so great was the power of his inspiration.

It was after about a month that things started to go wrong. His dreams had not always followed the course a Jeffery Farnol novel would have taken but, at least, promised a suitable ending. That now seemed to change. Too often his heroine would find herself in danger; too frequently the stress of office life was reflected in his dreams. So often that the novel acquired a darkness his inclination did not dictate. And, somehow, he was compelled to write. More and more his writing urge in the morning, still as strong, indeed becoming even stronger, cast dark shadows on the page, and infected its characters with gloom, malevolence and hatred. Completely unintentionally, his book began to acquire the nature of a Greek tragedy.

And his influence waned. He could not control his creations. His desire to pull them out of their world of gloom was not strong enough. They had taken over, had acquired lives of their own. He held the pen, but he was powerless to influence what he wrote.

It was affecting his life; it was affecting his work.

One Saturday, as he wrote in the garden, Adeline appeared at the door.

'I haven't got a package,' she said brightly.

'No, no; come in.'

'I'd love a cup of tea.'

'Oh, yes, tea. I'll put the kettle on.'

They walked into the garden.

'You have changed,' Adeline said.

Felix knew it. He knew why. He thrust a sheaf of papers at her – and the clipboard, which represented his morning's additions to the narrative.

She began to read. As she did so, her smile disappeared. She read to the end of the typescript, and then the scribbled continuation – and the notes for the development of the story. She looked pityingly at Felix.

'Oh, dear,' she said, 'I really intended…'

'That I should write a satisfactory ending?'

Adeline nodded.

'I cannot control my characters. They go their own way. It's as if I'm simply recording what is going on in another world. Well, anyway, I must get on – weekends are when I write most.'

Adeline felt she was being dismissed:

'Did you want another cup? I can make it.'

Felix shook his head. It was as if Adeline had ceased to exist. She walked towards the house. She was sure that he had not noticed her go; perhaps had forgotten she had come. She let herself out.

Felix's grim demeanour – so different from normal – was noticed. At the office, and wherever else he went, he began to be avoided. He cast a spell of despondency. But Adeline did not avoid him. She tried to improve his mood, but he was not to be lifted out of it.

And one day he finished his novel. Adeline did not like to ask how it had ended although she did discover that he had taken up reading again. While his writing had occupied so much of his life, he had found himself with little time for his erstwhile greatest pleasure. And he could now anticipate the end of books so vividly that he would often avoid struggling on to the end – adding to that 'special' shelf so frequently that he started another. He seemed to be able to predict more clearly whether the final pages would bring happiness for its characters, chiefly its hero or heroine, and did not risk the probability that they suffered an unpleasant fate.

Felix's life became a series of unfinished matters. Only a book designed for amusement could be finished and his mood would not entertain comedy – or even mild mirth.

Adeline had never been encouraged by Felix; he had never shown affection and she was unaware whether he felt any. But she could not take the view that others did – that Felix had made his bed and should, however uncomfortably, lie on it. She thought she should test him, see whether he would react to real life rather than live in an increasingly fictional one.

And she did.

Again she rang his bell on a bright weekend.

She sat with him in his sunny garden and tempted him with light conversation.

Noticing a book lying on the bench beside him, she reached over him to pick it up.

'Don't damage the spine,' he warned.

She held it carefully.

'*Three Men in a Boat*,' she read from the cover. 'I like Jerome K Jerome, particularly that one.'

'I've read it before, but I don't seem to be enjoying it so much this time.'

'I love the bit where he suffers every ailment known to man,' she laughed. 'Really funny.'

'Yes, yes,' he said. 'Amusing.'

She placed the book back by his side, deliberately touching his bare arm as she did so.

He stared ahead of him, as if waiting for her to go.

Instead she took his hand in hers.

'You know I'm really very fond of you.' She looked up into his eyes so that he could not avoid her gaze.

'Sort of, well, love you really.'

Felix looked at her, amazed. Here was a pretty girl – no, a beautiful girl, telling him that she loved him. Suddenly the sun burst out from a cloud which had temporarily hidden it. He looked at her more intently. Only she filled his mind. It was as if he had noticed her for the first time.

'I feel a fool,' he said.

She tightened her grasp on his hand and placed a kiss on his cheek. His vista was filled with her lovely face. Her arms came gently round him.

'You can tell me to go away,' she said. Then she laughed: 'You don't have to put up with this.'

He smiled. Then he laughed. Then he embraced her, took her head on his breast and wept.

'I feel a fool,' he said.

'Oh, now, you're becoming gloomy again.' But she was laughing as she said it. She dried his eyes.

Adeline did not discover whether his novel had a suitably happy ending until she bought a copy on a bookstall. But now it didn't matter. Happy ending or not, it became a lively seller.

Felix had started to take books off his 'unfinished' shelves and read to the end.

When Adeline called with a copy of his novel, he laughed: 'I could have given you a copy.'

'And lost a sale?'

He turned to her, took her hands in his and said:

'Sales? Success? Work? Play? Nothing matters any more.'

She waited for him to continue:

'Except you.'

The Ghost Road

It was the long commute to London that I loathed; every day the procession of villages, slowly being by-passed by the uniformity and mundanity of the A21. I was always relieved when I reached Hurst Green for I knew that Battle was just over the hill and home only thirty minutes away.

Always the same, driving the route had become mechanical and often induced in me a soporific effect – worryingly so.

It was late in November that I first started seeing 'the road', a turning off the main road which should not have been there. But it seemed real and I imagined – or was it that I saw them? – the tail lights of cars going down it. Sometimes the A21 seemed normal; at others I saw what I began, in my mind, to call the 'ghost road'.

It disturbed me; it led me to visit the reference library and search the Internet. With some concern I read of accidents – of cars which had swerved off the main road. I was unable, from these stories, to locate the exact place, but I believed it clear that some drivers had turned off believing a road to be there – and paid the price. Few were first hand experiences; one imagined that few who had made the turning had survived to relate their experiences later. There were too many vague tales and conjecture in the accounts of drivers taking the ghostly road.

I felt it was absurd: I was tired, irritable and thinking of my work, until I began to see the road more clearly. I studied current maps in the reference library. No such road existed. I went back and studied historical Ordnance Survey maps from the early nine-teenth century, closer to the time when the A21 was constructed in 1710. None showed me what I wanted – but dreaded – to see. A road that would restore my belief in my sanity.

Of course, I argued, my sanity had never been called into question. But I began to consider taking another route. Why should I do that? Was I to be taken well out of my way in order to avoid a road which, in my lucid moments, I believed did not exist. But the 'road' was beginning to affect my work – and my home life.

November eased into December and the weather was largely unremarkable but, on *the* night there was a gale-force wind playing with the car and blowing sheets of rain onto the wind-screen, making vision difficult.

I was approaching the point at which I had seen the road - which I still believed to be a figment of my imagination. And then I saw a car ahead. Vision prevented me from clearly seeing the direction I should be taking – despite my having travelled the road so often that I believed I could navigate it with my eyes shut. The road stretched ahead, the car's rear, red lights in front of me. I peered through the windscreen and hit the bank at the side of the road.

The car slid and, seeing another car's headlights bearing down on me, I swerved to the left. I turned in front of the ap-proaching car and assumed later that it had been able to slow to avoid hitting mine. I wrenched the steering wheel again and, de-spite a tearing of metal, avoided what could have been a fatal colli-sion.

In Hurst Green, I slowed and stopped at the side of the road to gather my wits and calm my shaken nerves. What returned to me was the recollection of the car ahead whose red rear lights I had followed. And the hideous face staring from its back window. What I could not forget was its grinning, toothless features, as if the face was enticing me forwards, determined that I should follow.

My life has changed since that day. I am lucky to be alive, and I realise just how close I had been to a hideous death.

And I have never driven that road since, preferring to take the train to London, hoping that I should not fall asleep and see, as I often did, the face of the devil in the car.

THE END